THE
HOUSE
OF BLUE
LIGHTS

THE
HOUSE
OF BLUE
LIGHTS

Robert J.
Bowman

ST. MARTIN'S PRESS
NEW YORK

Lyrics from "Choo Choo Ch'Boogie," by Vaughn Horton, Denver Darling, and Milton Gabler. Copyright © 1945 Rytvoc Inc. Copyright © renewed 1973 Rytvoc Inc. International copyright secured. All rights reserved. Used by permission.

Lyrics from "Drinkin' Wine, Spo-Dee-O-Dee, Drinkin' Wine," by Granville "Stick" McGhee and Mayo Williams. Copyright © 1949, 1973 by MCA Music Publishing, a division of MCA Inc., New York, NY. Copyright renewed. All rights reserved. Used by permission.

Lyrics from "The House of Blue Lights," by Don Raye and Freddie Slack. Copyright © 1946. Copyright © renewed 1978 Robbins Music Corp. All rights of Robbins Music Corp. assigned to SBK Catalog Partnership. All rights of Robbins Music Corp. controlled and administered by SBK Robbins Catalog. Used by permission.

Design by Martha Schwartz

Library of Congress Cataloging in Publication Data

Bowman, Robert.
   The house of blue lights.

   I. Title.
PS3552.08758H6   1987   813'.54   87-16380
ISBN 0-312-01042-7

First Edition

10 9 8 7 6 5 4 3 2 1

This is for Therese

Many thanks to E. J. Muller and Erik S. McMahon for their valuable editorial advice on an early draft of the manuscript.

Behold, I have graven thee upon the palms of my hands; thy walls are continually before me.

—Isaiah 49:16

Part One

1

It wasn't the clothes that set him apart from your average derelict. They were standard-issue, South of Market material: a greasy polyester blazer of green and white hound's-tooth check, golfer's pants in powder blue and lemon plaid, a maroon dress shirt, and a clumsily knotted tie emblazoned with big, bold paisleys swimming in a sea of electric orange. Nor was it his behavior—manic-depressive, but deadened by just enough lithium to keep him out of an institution. He was under control, for the time being. None of these details made him unique, provided he kept to the dozen or so blocks that served as San Francisco's dumping ground for its bums and crazies. What was different about him was the handcuffs.

Made of shiny tin or aluminum, they looked to be part of a Wild West Sheriff or Super Secret Agent kit. One cuff encircled his bony wrist. The other was clamped to a battered briefcase. He dialed the combination lock with shivering fingers and burrowed into the case. The contents rattled. Then came the felt pens.

There were dozens of them, each a different color, spilling onto the desk. He kept trying to arrange them in some mysterious order. Aqua, mauve, crimson, chartreuse—who made felt pens in so many colors? I was beginning to feel queasy. There was something about the decisions he was making—lima-bean green beside a washed-out peach, then a shade of pink reminiscent of fish drying in the sun. I was going to ask him about the pens when he started pulling out the charts.

These were an intricate network of notes, timetables, and diagrams running over sheets of graph paper held together by smudged Scotch tape. He had color-coded bar graphs, plotting graphs, curve graphs, pie charts, even a sheet of drawings that looked like storyboards for a movie. He unfolded them before me as if they were pieces of velvet protecting the most valuable diamonds in the world. "Do you have an easel that I can put these on?" he asked.

I stared at the Technicolor presentation. A typical Friday afternoon around the Hall of Justice. The accused start to get paranoid about being locked up until Monday. And the bums, facing two days without targets for spare change, step up their demands. Whether they're winos or psychos or addicts, or just lonely, their quirks become magnified, and it's best to get away early. I had been out of the San Francisco public defender's office for nearly a year, but a nine-year habit dies hard.

In a way this Friday was even worse. It was Labor Day weekend, when the employed, sick of a summer of San Francisco fog, flee the city to the homes of friends who enjoy normal weather patterns. The bums are left to their own devices. Worried that their favorite liquor stores won't be open on Monday, they start to panic.

On the Friday of the Felt Pens I had stretched out lunch to the point where it was acceptable, at least in my own mind, to go home. I had only returned to my temporary "office" in an alley across the street from the Hall to get my jacket, so when Adrian from the bail bond agency said that "something weird" was waiting upstairs, I seriously considered doing without it. After all, I was looking forward to something more than a long weekend. I had finally closed out the handful of cases that had come my way in recent weeks, mostly from Sonia Baine and a few other P.D.s. My

4

stint as an "investigator" was drawing to an end, along with the summer.

Perfect timing, as far as I was concerned. The lease of an office on Bail Bond Row from Art Shade ("Looking for a Bailout? It's Made in the Shade") was month to month, and my thirty days' notice of vacancy had been served that morning. A ready-made probate practice was waiting in Santa Rosa. Sara Ludlow, one of my professors at the University of San Francisco, had offered a partnership. It's not difficult choosing between the South of Market filth and a quiet job in a law firm where most of your clients are dead people. In my final days in the city, every bizarre new character who came to me hoping I could save his miserable ass was another obstacle to escaping from beneath the rock.

"These charts represent the evidence," he explained, awkwardly trying to position a piece of cardboard folded in thirds. It was like a science-fair project. "And here is the timetable." This was another taped-together construct with notes entered in a tiny hand beside columns separating the hours of the day. A different color of pen was used for each column. His hands trembled as he passed the document across the desk. "I have based it on the twenty-four-hour clock, Greenwich mean time. That is *atomic* time, you can get it on the radio. I have documentation of everyone who went in and everyone who went out—who he saw and what he did. Of course I may have missed something when I had to line up for dinner. My operatives are unreliable. I am the only one I can trust—excepting yourself, of course."

"Gee, these are real nice, Mr. . . ."

"Tuttle." He pushed his inch-thick glasses, the crosspiece thickened with electrical tape, back into place. "Sherman Tuttle."

He looked all around the ten-foot-square room before producing a stack of Polaroids bound by a dozen rubber bands. Removing them one by one, he fanned out the photos on the desk. "His name is Michael Patrick Sloane, the silent fister. He runs the shelter. I cannot tell you how I came to suspect him, but I am beginning to learn exactly what goes on there. It is . . . hideous."

"Michael Sloane?" The blurry photographs did show Sloane and some men in suits in front of The Wayside, his community shelter and dining room for South of Market's destitute. I knew him well—Michael was another former teacher of mine, in the Urban Studies Department at Berkeley. We had dated a couple of times after I graduated. Michael had arrived from back East sixteen years ago, starting a shelter in an abandoned warehouse with almost no money, what few funds there were coming from his teaching job and a smattering of community donations. Naturally, he had made an army of enemies—but all from the world of big business and city politics. Somebody was always complaining that Michael was competing with the respectable charities. It was unusual for one of his "guests," if that is what Sherman Tuttle was, to turn against him.

Tuttle nodded with vigor. "I cannot tell you everything yet. Someday it will all come out. But I will say this." He leaned closer. I expected the waft of alcohol, but it didn't come. "They are conducting *experiments*."

This was the place for a prompt. "Experiments?"

He took a breath. "You must help me, Miss Thorpe. They have gone can-kicky; they will not let me inside anymore. Of course they know I am on to them; that is to be expected— but there is so much more to learn. Many, many details. That is why I came to you. Don't turkey-neck. Make yourself invisible, reconnoiter, and report back. I will do the rest."

"I've never been very good at disappearing." He'll never go away, I despaired.

My impatience must have been obvious, for Tuttle straightened up, offended. "You will just have to trust me, like I am trusting you." Then he leaned in again. "Suffice to say . . . I know the Kennedys."

There was a time when a nut like Tuttle would have won my sympathy. Now it was impossible to recall how I had ever summoned up the patience and understanding. There are so many like him, I thought, their minds destroyed by

6

drugs, by poverty—by birth. Only the symptoms vary. How can I possibly help him?

"Mr. Tuttle . . . please understand, I'm real busy right now." Nice try, Cass. I groped for another excuse, then made the mistake. "And I doubt you can afford me."

It would have been better to tell the truth: I'm not really an investigator, I'm closing the office, I'm leaving town, and I'm never coming back. Tuttle reached into his bottomless briefcase and withdrew a wad of money. They must have handed out the disability checks early. He started riffling through the bills. "What is your fee?" he asked primly. "Your daily rate, plus expenses? And I assume there is a bonus, if you get results?"

"Put the money away." Enough was enough. "Look, Mr. Tuttle. I'm sorry, but I'm not taking any cases right now. And I certainly can't take your money." I pushed the mass of papers, photos, and pens toward him. A couple of pens rolled off the desk and he dove for them. I leaned over to see him scrambling on his knees, his nose to the floor to compensate for poor vision. He needed one hand just to hold his glasses on. Finally he located the stray pens and resurfaced. He stared at me, slack-jawed, for a long time, eyes magnified by the thick glasses. Eventually a look of comprehension crossed his face, and he smiled.

"Underst," he whispered, gathering his possessions with shaky hands. It was nice to know that one of us did. "I will be in touch—when it is safer to talk." The briefcase snapped shut. He took a neatly folded piece of notebook paper from his coat pocket and placed it before me.

He said not another word as he hugged the briefcase, pushed at his glasses one final time, and slunk out. I followed him to the door, just in case he decided to turn around and occupy one of my chairs for another half hour. But he kept going. He disappeared around the first turn of the stairs without looking back.

Seconds later he cried out from the stairwell. "Aaaargh," said a voice. "Get away from me!" Tuttle shrieked. Then someone went clumping down the stairs.

Thirty seconds passed. Finally, a face emerged at the turn

7

of the stairs—or rather half a face, peeking around the corner. The face was grinning, the mouth half open and leaking a thread of drool. "Aargh," said the face. Then it emerged into full view.

"Hellooo, sweetie," the bum leered. It was Elroy, the *de facto* mascot of the public defender's office. He was a black man of indeterminate age, and his appearance to the uninitiated was genuinely horrific: no front teeth, filthy khaki pants, unraveling cardigan sweater, and shoes without laces. Officially, he was paid a dollar a week to sweep the P.D.'s offices, provided he could stay sober, but he had enough sources of income to afford a bottle of something every few days. He would use the cash to go on periodic binges, which generally ended in his getting beaten up by somebody, punching out an old lady or a cop, and landing in jail. After spending anywhere from twenty-four hours to six months behind bars, he would be cut loose miserably sober, at which time I would give him all the change in my purse and he would proceed to get drunk again at the earliest possible moment. He was convinced that I was his wife.

He took two tottering steps. "Elroy," I said sternly, "you're off limits." We had an agreement that he was never to enter the office above the bailbondsman.

"Aargh," he repeated. "Mmph garr aahoo ra argh ten dollars?" The crucial words always came out crystal clear.

He climbed four more steps. Kissing range. I ducked back into the office and grabbed my purse, pulling out a dollar bill. Returning to the stairwell, I held it out to him. He stretched as far as he could without having to advance, and just managed to snatch the money away. "Sweetie, I looove your curly hair!" he cried before disappearing.

I went inside to retrieve my empty briefcase. On the desk was the slip of paper that Sherman Tuttle had left behind. CASSANDRA THORPE, PRIVATE INVESTIGATOR, it said, followed by my address. Somebody has a sense of humor.

The office window faced away from the Hall of Justice, away from that wall of battleship gray and the winos of Bryant Street. I looked out on Potrero Hill, where I lived, with its old houses, warehouses, and trendy design studios, and a factory stack that emitted smoke around the clock. That smoke looked different every day—sometimes a massive black cloud, other times a wisp. Today a plume of white disappeared into the late-summer sun. Foghorns boomed in the distance. The shadows were getting longer. In the back-yard below, a ratty Scottish terrier was asleep on the lawn.

Rising to leave at last, I saw that a felt pen had rolled under the desk. Day-Glo orange.

2

"It won't play nothin' but that goddamn punk crap of Bernard's. Your mother can't even get her opera out of it no more."

Joseph loomed over me as I examined the innards of the jukebox at my mother's Italian restaurant in San Francisco's North Beach. It was one of those colorless, late-model Rock-Olas that carve a ditch in every record they play, and it had taken a beating.

"Tone arm's stuck," I said. "Probably from too much grease. I told you to move it away from the grill."

"Hey, be careful, that's Waylon on there." Joseph used his fingernail to scrape a bit of spaghetti sauce off the glass. Because he could fix virtually anything else, he was forever frustrated over his ignorance of the machine. He was head chef, office manager, wine captain, bouncer, master electrician, and plumber, and it took every bit of gentlemanly grace he possessed to defer to me in the matter of the jukebox. "Goddamn junkbox, that's what it is. Really burns my ass. You gonna be able to fix it?"

"I'll scrounge around for parts at home," I said, hanging the well-used OUT OF ORDER sign over the coin slot. The condition of the jukebox could only help the atmosphere at the Nick of America. In its working hours the machine was a constant source of bickering among the staff, my mother preferring opera, Joseph country-western, and Bernard, the busboy, punk. If nobody was paying attention, I would occasionally punch up some rock and roll or rhythm and blues, but mostly I stayed out of the music wars.

"Joseph, I need you at the grill," my mother called out from behind the steaming pots and pans. If Joseph was the brains and muscle of the restaurant, she was its heart and nerve center—somehow managing to be everywhere at once, greeting customers, manning the register, and juggling twenty orders in her head without writing down a single one. An Irishwoman running an Italian restaurant, she was a neighborhood miracle.

Everyone said I was like my mother, on the outside at least: taller than I wanted to be, thick auburn hair that I wished were darker, pale complexion that I wished were swarthier, brown eyes, high forehead. That part I liked—it made me look smart.

Joseph strolled back to the grill and fired up another batch of calamari, the Friday-night special. It was only 5:30, and people wouldn't be lining up on the sidewalk for another hour or so. I was headed for a booth when Sonia Baine walked in.

"Smooth move," she said, peering over her glasses in mock reproach. "There I am, all ready to unload another batch of cases. And you take off early. Nice try."

Sonia, a five-foot-ten black woman, was an inch shorter than me, but she made me feel dwarfed. Reared in a family of gospel singers, she knew how to command the attention of a jury. Yet I had never heard her utter a swearword. She had a large frame, although she wasn't fat, and the best posture of anyone I knew.

Sonia slid into the booth across from me, dumping a stack of files on the tabletop.

"You are going to love these. One guy flashed right in front of the Ukrainian church. That's the same character who almost gave that little old lady a heart attack? Then another one came to court last week dressed like a *frogman,* if you can picture it. Mask, flippers, the works. And the usual half-dozen small-time dope deals. Mostly in the projects, I'm sure you know what that means."

"Boudeaux."

"Too right." Louis Boudeaux was behind most of the drug cases handled by the P.D.'s office, but he was seldom charged for them, let alone convicted. His "lieutenants" took the rap. On the few occasions that Boudeaux was up for minor charges, he never stooped to the use of a public defender.

"Look them over and tell me what you want," said Sonia, rummaging in her purse for a cigarette. "Every one needs a crack investigator." I glanced through the stack, an encyclopedia of the lower forms of life. Lewd and lascivious, breaking and entering, drunk and -disorderly, pimping and pandering. . . .

I pushed the files away. "I don't want any of them."

"Picky, picky. Well how about this one? A gentleman who copulates with dogs while singing the theme song from 'Petticoat Junction.' You know?" She started to sing, and when she got to the part about Uncle Joe a-movin' kinda slow, I stopped her.

"Enough!"

"What's the matter, you didn't like that show?"

"That's not what I meant and you know it. The office is closed for good. Lost Our Lease."

She sighed. "What *do* you want to leave this lovely city for, anyway?" It was a familiar question from people who didn't spend much time South of Market, but Sonia knew better. In our San Francisco there was no Fisherman's Wharf, no Coit Tower or sourdough bread. Just people in breadlines who couldn't afford the dollar cable car ride to Ghirardelli Square. And if they had the money, they were more likely to spend it on a bottle of Thunderbird.

"You should talk," I said. "You live in San Mateo."

"Really, Cass, come on. You've got to help me out. The flasher's on calendar for Wednesday? And the 211 could go next week too. It's only a couple days' work and there's not enough time to get it to the investigators and you *know* they'd mess it up anyway. Then think how bad you'd feel."

"Will you stop it with the guilt?" She was doing her polite pit bull act. With Sonia, everything was an obligation, a moral crusade that would collapse without my participation. It was like trying to reason with a nun.

My mother came over with two plates of calamari. "Eat up. We're going to run low tonight."

"Why, thank you, Mrs. Mastrangelo," Sonia said sweetly, clearing a space for the food. My mother didn't go away. She was looking at the files with unconcealed disapproval.

"Thanks, Mama." Still she didn't move.

"Lots of work tonight," she finally said to me.

"Um, no, it's Sonia's. She wanted some help, and I was just telling her no when you walked up." I turned to Sonia. "No." Then back to my mother. "See?"

She shook her head and walked away. "I'll bring over some wine."

"Oh, good," Sonia said to me. "Then I can get you drunk and change your foolish mind."

"I heard that," my mother said.

It was my mother's belief that I should never have become a public defender and mixed with the "unsavory elements." If her daughter was going to be a lawyer, she would tell her friends, why couldn't she get into business law or tax law, and help out the family? Naturally she was overjoyed when she heard of Sara Ludlow's offer. None of this was ever said to me directly. Each of my mother's statements required five more links in the chain of logic before the point was revealed.

Sonia waited for her to get out of earshot. "Now where were we? You were showing distinct interest in the man who loves dogs, saying it's right down your alley—"

"I was saying nothing of the sort! You can't talk me into anything. Which reminds me." I showed her the scrap of paper with my name and address on it, Sherman Tuttle's parting gift. "You?"

She feigned ignorance, then slapped her forehead. "You know? I guess I did send him over."

"And why, may I ask, did you do that?"

"He was just a poor old crazy man, you can see that for

yourself. With no priors, and he seemed so . . . helpless. So I thought, why not keep him out of the system?"

"Are we thinking of the same guy here? I mean, we're talking handcuffs and briefcases and *lots* of felt pens, right?"

She grimaced, her mouth full of calamari. "Yeah, that *is* the one."

"What a prize. He'll be going along sounding perfectly coherent, then suddenly he'll lapse into baby talk. It's unnerving."

"Like goo-goo ga-ga?"

"No, more semi-nonsense. Like they're almost words, but they're not. Anyway, it sounds like he's been giving Michael a hard time."

"Uh-huh. It was Michael who had him arrested for trespassing, you know."

"I can't say I blame him. If I saw this 'poor old crazy man' following me, I might call the cops, too. And what's this 'Private Investigator' crap anyway?" I held up the paper again. "You realize I could get in a lot of trouble for practicing without a license?"

"Well, I had to call you something. That was the whole point. Send the man to a professional. That is, unless you're planning on coming back to the P.D.'s."

I just shook my head. Every once in a while Sonia would try that. She was the only one who dared.

"Okay, okay. Forget it. You're probably smart not to get involved." Sonia stabbed another calamari with her fork and contemplated the wriggling tentacles. "I'll just have to do my best to keep him out of jail."

"He's not in jail, last time I looked. Who bailed him out, anyway?"

"Michael did."

"What!"

Sonia pushed the stack of files over to me. "Look, just pick *one* teeny little case out of here for me. I'll go play the jukebox while you decide which one."

"What are you talking about?"

"I just *know* I've got a quarter here somewhere. What do you want to hear?"

14

"It's out of order."

"Then let's go over to Roma's and shoot some pool. They've got a jukebox there that works."

"Sonia, will you please explain why Michael Sloane bailed out the same guy he had arrested?"

"Girl, it is Friday night. Now get out of that booth and start having fun before I break your arm."

3

Actually, the story wasn't too difficult to figure out, even if Sonia refused to discuss it for the rest of the evening. It had all the earmarks of one of Michael Sloane's schemes: ridiculous, manipulative, and effective. Perhaps Sherman Tuttle *would* be happy if he believed he had hired a private eye to follow up one of his paranoid delusions. Where was the harm in it, if even the target of those delusions considered him harmless?

Fine in theory, but I had no intention of being roped in. Nothing would keep me in the city longer than working for Michael. And there was a risk to my own reputation. Until now my investigative work had been restricted to public defender cases, handled on a very "unofficial" basis. Suddenly I was being advertised as a "private investigator," if only to a lunatic. It couldn't be more different from what I intended to do with my life. I had to say no.

How to say it was another problem. Realizing that I would have to face Michael at some point, I gave in to Sonia's request that I show up the next morning at a meeting of the Neighborhood Coalition. Known simply as "the Neighborhood," they were opposing the big developers South of Market, and Michael was one of their leaders. When the meeting was over, I would tell him.

The Neighborhood convened at a church that ran one of the area's less popular shelters. Built forty or fifty years ago, it had somehow managed to stave off the bulldozers when everything from liquor stores to old people's homes was being flattened to make way for the convention center. The bums wouldn't have minded seeing it go. They had to endure a fiery sermon before sitting down to their gruel, and the Protestant work ethic demanded that they pitch in on cleanup afterward. The Cleveland Memorial Baptist Church would rate barely a star in the Official Triple-A Guide to Flophouses.

Michael was addressing a group of about sixty when Sonia and I showed up. Dressed in his trademark work shirt and blue jeans, he was pacing the pulpit, raised up on his toes to compensate for the fact he was only five feet five inches tall.

"If you just stand in their way," he was saying, "you force 'em to roll right over you. And believe me, they won't be willing to pay that price. Meaning tons of bad publicity. Endless permit delays. And money, money, money. But give 'em the chance to move in on the area? They'll take it. Every time they'll take it. Am I right?"

A murmur of approval rose from the audience.

"Well, what are you going to do about it? Just sit there nodding your heads all day and smiling, saying, 'Yeah, tell it, brother, you're right'? Or get up off your collective ass and *fight* this thing?"

He was just warming up, starting in a soft, conversational tone and building from there, preacher style. Appropriate for a Protestant church. It wasn't the words that got results; it was the emotion behind them. By the time he was done, he would have these people on their feet, headed for the barricades. Once I might have followed. The prospect of a political fight, a court battle, even a tough pretrial motion, used to get my blood rushing. Now the rush was gone. Drained away.

"Okay, people, we're setting up some committees, and I want everybody to put their name on at least one of the sign-up sheets outside the door when we're done here. . . ."

There were doughnuts and coffee in the vestibule, and I

17

sought them out. Two bums were bent over the doughnut table. One wore a stocking cap and tattered peacoat, the other several sweatshirts and camouflage pants. The first was saying, "You, you, you, you could get a *glazed* doughnut."

"Don't want no *glazed* doughnut," said the other man. "Can't take the sugar content, understand?"

"You, you, you could have a glazed *old-fashioned*. Or get you a buttermilk with some speckles on it."

"I'm tellin' you 'bout the *sugar*, man. Just like in the wine, you know. It make me puke."

"It ain't the *wine* that make you do that, it's what you *eat!*"

The second bum noticed me standing in the doorway. Glaring at me, he stuffed his pockets with doughnuts, and the two of them shuffled out. "Now your cheese danish is another matter *entirely* . . ." the second one was saying. I helped myself to a cup of coffee.

Finally the sound of applause came from within, and people began filing into the vestibule. Michael emerged, accompanied by Sonia and two or three of his aides-de-camp. He was deep in conversation, laying out plans for the latest assault on the developers.

Michael saw me standing by the doughnuts and, dismissing all but Sonia, came over. He was a slightly built man in his early forties, although his dark, bushy hair was still thick and his waist was still thin. The lines etched around his eyes and mouth were transforming his boyish good looks into a rugged handsomeness. It was a face you could take seriously.

"Sorry to drag you into a heathen church," he said with a grin.

"They're all the same to me."

"Oh. Right. Well, then, it's all in the line of duty."

"What duty might that be?"

"Me. My case. Checking up on my every move. You're probably getting ready to file your first report. Anything I can do to help out? Get you an itinerary or something?" As usual, Michael's words came out like machine-gun fire.

"I happen to be unemployed right now."

"She's playing hard to get," said Sonia.

Michael popped a piece of glazed doughnut into his mouth. "I realize the job seems a bit unusual."

18

"Just a tad. But it could be the most routine assignment in the world and I still wouldn't take it. Even if it *weren't* offered under false pretenses."

"So you're right about that. I should have been straight with you. But I was afraid you wouldn't take the case."

"A lot of good it did," I said. "Are you aware of what this guy's saying about you?"

"Sure. There's spacemen, KGB agents, and nuclear weapons hidden all over the place. Look—I'll admit I overreacted when I had him arrested. But he was getting to be a damned pest, sneaking in after hours, spying around. The other day I caught him in my office, taking pictures of a *plant*, for godsake. Maybe he thought I had a microphone hidden in the thing."

"Did you?"

He chose to ignore the crack. "But then I cooled down, and I said to myself, what do we have here? The guy's a nut, but he's harmless. So I got to thinking we ought to be able to help him somehow. Sure, I could have dropped the case and forgotten the whole thing, but he would have gone after someone else and ended up in jail. I mean, let's face it. He doesn't need ninety days in county; he needs someone to shrink his head for him."

"I'm not for hire on this one."

Michael shook his head and gave me one of his I'm-extremely-disappointed-with-you-Cass looks. "You're getting cynical in your retirement, Thorpe. I suppose this is all part of the master plan to run away to Santa Rosa and vegetate? You know you can't get away from crazy people up there, don't you?"

"I am not getting away from *anything*." Michael had an infuriating way of putting you on the defensive—part of the style that helped him push people around at the highest levels of business and politics. And he never lost an argument: intimidation through guilt.

This time, though, he seemed to be giving in. "Fine, you win," he sighed. "It was just an idea. And I've got a more interesting job for you anyway."

"Michael, I didn't turn down Tuttle because he wasn't *interesting* enough."

"Take a look. Tell me what you think." Michael withdrew from his back pocket a torn-off piece of paper that had been balled up and uncrumpled several times. "The other night somebody put this through the mail slot at The Wayside."

I had to smooth the sheet to make out the narrow pencil marks. There was no salutation, no date. I AM COMING BACK, it read. TELL NO ONE. I WILL BE COMING BACK FOR MY TRESHURE. HELP ME.

The signature was printed as well: TOMMY MALAKIS.

I handed the note back. "So?"

"So," Michael said, "do you believe in ghosts?"

"Why?"

"Because I personally signed his death certificate thirteen years ago."

4

Saturday was floor-mopping day at The Wayside. Michael had three bums doing the job. They were leaning on their mops for support, and the cots were getting as wet as the floors, but their dedication was evident. That night they would get the best beds in the house, and maybe a couple of packs of cigarettes on the sly.

"Oh, Saerncisco's okay," one of the moppers was saying to the others. "Better'n a lotta places. Can't freeze to death at night. Never get hot enough to kill you with sunstroke. Only problem's the damp, I mean the fog, and the earthquakes. They say the whole damn city's gonna plop into the sea one day, in a piece. That don't scare me. That's something that *might* happen, as against what *is*. Me, I'll just wait around for the quake."

We picked our way through the pools of soapy water. "Looking good, Sal!" Michael called out to the bum who had spoken. Actually, the place looked pretty good to begin with, at least by South of Market standards. There were two large rooms, one for dining and the other for sleeping. The sixty-odd cots were neatly made—that was a requirement for getting out of the place in the morning—and a waft of disinfectant masked the more offensive odors. The code of behavior was engraved on hand-printed signs hung on the walls like art: THIS IS YOUR HOME—TREAT IT LIKE ONE; WATCH YOUR PROPERTY; VIOLENCE WILL NOT BE TOLERATED—LEAVE IT AT THE DOOR. The Wayside was stark, but it was warm, and better than a cardboard box.

Over the entrance was a wooden plaque with a picture of a spreading oak tree and the word SAFEPLACE beneath it. Michael had posted this symbol all over South of Market and the Tenderloin; it meant that here was a place where the old or weak could escape from the jackals out on the street. Safeplaces were hotels, apartment buildings, shelters, churches, even some liquor stores—wherever there was a proprietor or building manager willing to offer sanctuary. If an old person was being harassed for his social security check or a wino was in danger of being rolled, he could take refuge there.

Michael led Sonia and me to his office, a small room in the back decorated with glossy color photographs of seascapes, mountainscapes, and other scapes of nonurban beauty. From the other room I could hear someone tooling around on the shelter's dilapidated upright piano. It was Early Times, or E.T., a bum who frequented The Wayside and some of the local bars, performing for a drink or a place to sleep. He was playing a desultory boogie-woogie.

Michael motioned us to some chairs—I got a carved-up wooden desk rejected from some elementary school years before. I had promised to listen to his story, although I couldn't say why. Maybe it was the challenge: there's no way Michael Sloane can force me to do anything, I thought. I'll show him. Now I was sitting in a child's school desk and facing my former college teacher. It felt more like the principal's office.

"The question is," said Michael, "who is Tommy Malakis?"

"I'm dying to know." Too much like the school kid. Shut up.

"Years ago," he continued, "he used to run a bar over on Barron near Second, the Leeward Inn. You've heard of it?"

I said I hadn't.

"Anyway. The bar burned down and he lost the property.

22

Couldn't collect on the insurance. It seems they think he might have torched the place himself, but they never proved it one way or the other."

"It wouldn't be the first time somebody tried that around here," said Sonia.

"Sort of instant urban renewal, yeah. Well, the cops came up blank, too. Some poor old wino died in the fire. Happened to be sleeping in the doorway. Malakis was in bed upstairs, but he got out in time."

I spoke up in spite of myself. "So what happened to him?"

"He hit the skids. Drifted from place to place, nobody paid much attention to him, the typical story. I put him up here for a week or so, till he split and started sleeping on the streets. He never stayed in one place for too long. Then one night he was murdered in Wino Park."

"Beaten?"

"Burned. Some maniac doused his sleeping bag with gasoline and lit a match. He was trapped."

"Just like his bar," I said. "But how did they know it was him?"

"It was my sleeping bag, or what was left of it. He borrowed it when he left The Wayside. One of those Smokey the Bear bags, you couldn't mistake it. He carried it everywhere. About all he had left. And he'd been sleeping in the exact same corner of the park for three nights running. All the bums swore to it. Anyway, the cops never solved the murder. I doubt they tried too hard."

"Where do you come in?"

"As usual, I was the only one who gave enough of a shit to make an I.D. Thought that would be the end of it. Just wanted to give the poor guy a decent burial."

"Sounds like you were wrong."

"I'd like to find out." He had the piece of paper in front of him, and was trying to iron out the creases.

"And now he's back from the dead and he wants *what*? What's this about a treasure?"

Michael rubbed the bridge of his nose. "Okay, there was some story back then about him having a lot of money buried underneath his bar. Or so he claimed. That's what the locals told the cops. The bar itself isn't there anymore. Right now it's a parking lot, and in a couple of years it's going to be part of that humongous hotel and office thing the Neighborhood's been trying to stop for the last two years. Sunrise City, they're calling it. Great view from there. The yuppies can watch the sun come up while they eat their croissants."

"Let me guess. And you think you can use this Malakis guy to help you stop the project."

"Bingo. He'd be a real wrench in the works. Here's a man who everybody thinks is dead, and suddenly maybe he's alive, and so is his claim to this piece of property, which may have a goddamn *treasure chest* buried under it. I mean, come on! The story could hold up construction for a year or more. Think how much it would cost the developers. Not to mention free publicity for us. We'd get the press, the Historical Society, the treasure hunters. . . . It'd be chaos!"

I felt a certain relief. It wasn't going to be difficult to turn down Michael this time. The scheme and the story behind it were just too farfetched to be taken seriously. I waited for him to crack a smile, or show some sign that he understood the absurdity of what he was saying.

I got tired of waiting. "So some guy comes up with a fairy tale to sell drinks and you think the Historical Society is going to turn an empty lot into a museum? I can see it now: 'Ladies and gentlemen, here is a perfect example of an old waterfront dive, circa mid-twentieth century. It's been restored right down to the beer bottles—'"

"That's the beauty of it," said Michael, who always had an answer for everything. "It doesn't matter if it's true. All we're trying to do at this point is stall the project. They've already got the permits. And if a dead guy comes back to life to claim his property, that's *news*, Cass! At the very least we'll buy some time."

"And at the very most?"

"We can shoot the whole damned thing to the ground." He was trembling with excitement over the prospect.

"Sonia," I said, "Michael *is* leading up to something here, isn't he?"

"Are you, Michael?" Sonia asked.

"I need you to find Tommy Malakis," Michael said.

Early Times picked up the boogie-woogie beat and started humming along. I found myself dreading the prospect of searching for this man in the skid row scum. The forest scene on Michael's wall looked like paradise. The music, rhythmic and irresistible, seemed to go with it. Get away from there, it said.

I said, "But if that letter really is from Malakis, that means *he* came to *you* in the first place. Why not just wait for him to show up at your door?"

"Three reasons. One, there's no guarantee he will. Two, we haven't got time to wait. Maybe he's in no hurry, but we are. We've got to find him before anyone else does."

"Who else? The evil developers?"

"Whoever. The plan is, find Malakis fast, keep him safe and under wraps, then spring him on the builders at the right moment."

"It's a great plan, really it is." I eased out of the tiny school desk. Keep him safe from what? A lousy property development company? It didn't make sense. "I wish I could help, but I can't. Just like with Sherman Tuttle. Now will you quit bugging me?" I was doing great.

"Two and a half weeks," Michael pleaded. "That's all we need. On the eighteenth the developers are going to hold a community meeting, where they plan to 'introduce' the project and convince us that we should tear up our plans for low-cost housing and make way for another goddamn hotel for creeps in white shoes. Imagine what would happen if we brought Malakis to that meeting. Anyway, if you haven't found him by that time and he hasn't shown up here, then you can forget the whole thing. It won't slow you down at all."

"But your connections are a lot better than mine." He's got me arguing with him again, damn it.

"Mine are too good. If they know I'm looking for Malakis, the whole thing will be public information in a second. But if *you* asked around the P.D.'s, the cops, the shelters—if you asked *quietly*—you just might come up with something."

In other words, if I stood on the rooftops and shouted the name of Tommy Malakis all over town. Quietly.

"Who owns the property now?" I asked.

"A group of investors out of Hong Kong. The usual faceless foreigners. They're represented by a management company here in town, Sunrise Development."

"Do you think he has any legal claims?"

"I don't know. Maybe. Probably not. But anything's worth a try."

"What's he look like thirteen years later? Do you have a photograph?"

Michael shook his head. "No pictures. As best I can remember . . . medium height, maybe five five, five six . . . heavyset, white hair. Old. I'll know him when I see him."

"Aren't you forgetting something?"

"What's that?"

"Tommy Malakis. Nobody's asked his opinion."

"Want to know the third reason why I don't sit on my ass until he walks through that door?" Michael waved the note at me. "I think he's scared shitless. Can't you just tell from reading this? Somebody's already tried to kill him. Who's to say he's not still around? You'd hide too, under the circumstances."

Afraid. Of course he was afraid. That was obvious. Somewhere out there was a nut who liked to set fire to people in sleeping bags. A psychopath hulking around in the dark. And Michael was kind enough to get Malakis a protector: me.

"No," I said.

Piece of cake. I headed for the door.

"Run away," Michael said.

"What?"

"Go on, run away. You're scared, I can tell."

"You can't goad me into this, Michael."

"Hey, I'm just telling you what I think. I know you. You're through with this crap, right? Just like everybody else. You go to college, talk big about defending the underdog. Oh yeah, I remember. All this noise about 'people ground down by the system' and 'victims of society.' Then you get burned, and suddenly you can't get up in front of a jury anymore. And now you want to get the hell out and hide away somewhere. Ex-P.D., ex-investigator, ex-Catholic—man, you're ex-everything, aren't you?"

"Michael, cut it out," Sonia warned.

"You want to run?" Michael asked me, ignoring Sonia. "Get away from the shit? Well, let me tell you something about that, Cass. It *finds* you. Maybe it even goes *with* you. And while you're trying to keep out of its way, the same ground-down people are still living in the same caves and gutters. But then I guess you're just too much of a fuck-up to help them anymore."

"How dare you talk to her like that!" Sonia cried out.

Control. Keep calm. That's the secret. That's my strength. I know what he's doing and I won't let him do it. The Barracuda, that's what they used to call me. The Control Freak. Show him.

"It's all right, Sonia," I said shakily. "This is Michael's idea of shock therapy. I'm supposed to get so pissed off at him that I'll take the case."

"Either that or she'll never speak to me again," Michael said.

I stood in the doorway and watched the bums moving across the floor with their mops in time to the rolling beat of the piano. I felt numb, as if I had just had four wisdom teeth pulled. Actually, Michael's psychology was ridiculously off base. He had made it almost impossible for me to accept. Assuming I had a shred of self-respect left, the only real option was to walk out the door.

"Two and a half weeks?" I asked him.

"Two and a half weeks."

"It's going to take longer than that just to check all the flophouses in the city."

"I'll get you a list."

"If I find him, I'll tell him you're looking for him. That's all."

"But we've got to know *where* he is. . . ."

"It's up to him. That's the best I can do for you."

I didn't say anything for a minute or two. In the other

room E.T. started singing, his cracked voice picking up volume as he played, first haltingly, then with confidence:

> You take a morning paper
>   from the top of the stack,
> And read the situations
>   from the front to the back,
> The only job that's open
>   needs a man with a knack,
> So put it right back in the rack, Jack.

Michael had won again, the bastard.

5

It was another sign of my fading dedication to the underclass that I hurried from The Wayside to make the final softball game of the season. The Nick of America—my mother's restaurant—was playing its arch-rival, the Columbus, out at Moscone Field in the Marina. They had thrashed us the season before, and the league trophy had been collecting enemy grease two blocks away for a year. I was expected to do my part to even the score, so I hunkered behind the plate and played punching bag for runners sliding home until they finally took me out of the game in the fourth inning. It was then that I saw, through a rapidly swelling eye, Sherman Tuttle, lurking behind the rotting wood grandstands. His orange and brown plaid pants shone through the spaces between the evergreen slats. He was just standing there, peering through those thick spectacles, willing me to him. Hardly a subtle approach: the plaids were shouting loud enough for everyone to hear.

I ambled over to the bleachers and sat so that our eyes would be at the same level. I leaned back and watched the action on the field.

"Buzzchick," he said as Joseph slammed the ball over the head of the Columbus center fielder. "Rude eye."

"Uh . . . how're you doing, Mr. Tuttle?"

"You are fired," he said.

I resisted the urge to turn around. "I'm sorry?"

"I know you have talked to that deejer Sloane. I know you went to see him. You are in league with him."

"Look, I wasn't even . . ."

"I have added you to the charts," he said darkly. "I am afraid I am going to have to take you off the case. I should have known from the start because everything is connected to everything else through an invisible web of circumstance. *You are one of his.*"

I didn't have time to say another word. "Remember the words of the prophets," Tuttle said, and then he was gone, leaving only the sound of running feet. Somebody had scared him away.

The somebody sidled up, taking Tuttle's place under the bleachers. Dark, greasy pompadour, nylon jacket with epaulets and sleeves pushed up to the elbows, white high-tops and T-shirt: a WASP from Marin County trying to pass as an Italian from Manhattan. It was Eddie, my ex-husband. He had an entirely different reason for hiding. Joseph had threatened to break his neck if he ever showed it around me again. He was taller than Tuttle, so I moved up a row.

"Wow. That was one strange dude. Who was he, anyway? He like booked the minute he saw me."

"Who can blame him?"

"I wanted to ask where he got those pants. Anyway, what were you two doing, having some kinda secret conversation? Looked like a payoff or something."

"No, I just like to come out here and talk to people who hide under the grandstands."

Eddie snickered. "Hey listen, I was in the neighborhood and got to wondering if you could help me out with a little favor. No big deal. Thought we might talk about it."

"You're talking."

"You weren't bad out there today. I was watching."

"Any chance of your getting to the point?" I wanted to put my eye on ice.

Eddie's hand emerged from beneath my seat, holding out a roll of 35-millimeter film. "Stash this for me, okay? Not long, but I gotta like get it off my person for a few days."

"You into porno now? Kids, dogs, that kind of thing?"

"Humorous, real humorous. It happens to be pretty important. I've been doing a little insurance stuff on the side, helping some people out. These are shots of a rear-ender over on Sixth Street the other day. I'm on the scene, you know, I'm gonna sell the guy in the second car my pictures so he'll have something to show his insurance company, right? All of a sudden the scumbags who caused the accident start like pushing me around."

"Let me guess. You took them both on and beat the shit out of them."

"Look, I only got outta there 'cause a cop showed up. But these guys, I think they know who I am, and I've got a feeling they won't give up on getting this film. My guess is, they're into some kinda insurance scam—you know, like braking all of a sudden and then suing the poor schmuck behind. . . . Like I said, it's no big deal. I just need some time for things to cool off."

Eddie laughed nervously. He had been "on the scene" of a lot of accidents lately, just happening to have a camera, a stack of business cards—and a police radio in his car. In a lot of cases, scared drivers had been happy to pay for his pictures in order to prove their claims, justified or not. This time he had shown up at the wrong accident.

Until now, this had been Eddie's most successful venture in a long time. After losing his job at the *San Francisco Herald,* where he was working as a photographer when I married him, he had drifted for a while, messing up in a variety of places. He now fancied himself a producer of documentaries, but was always taking odd jobs while "waiting for the budget to come in." Prior to going into business as an ambulance chaser, he had driven one of those pilot cars that guide wide-load trucks on the freeways. The first time, he lost the truck. The second time he ran into it.

"I'll do it," I said, "if you do something for me."

"Oh, sure, there's always a catch. Remember last time? I almost got killed by that garbage truck. So if it means rummaging through scummy trash cans again, you can forget about it."

"Actually, it's nothing like that. You've still got a friend on the police force, don't you?"

"Yeah, I met this guy while I was working for the paper . . . I guess he's still there."

"I need a couple of police reports." I gave him Malakis's name, and the dates of the fire and the incident in Wino Park, but little else by way of explanation. "And Eddie—this is the most important thing."

"Yeah?"

"Keep your mouth shut about this."

"Who you think you're dealing with here?" The hand reappeared. I took the roll of film.

"Hey, Cass, you're a detective, maybe you can help me with this idea I got. We're doing this documentary on Marilyn Monroe, the real story and all that. I'm thinking I'll have this private eye who's on the trail of the truth—you know, like what was she *really* like? You can fill in the little bits of color, like how the guy would act and everything. He's got the trench coat, the hat. . . . This producer in Hollywood, he loves the idea, he says send him a treatment, we could work on it together—oh, shit."

The mood was broken by Joseph's voice and the sight of the big man lumbering over to the stands. "Be talking to you," Eddie mumbled before running off.

Joseph clambered up the shaky structure to my row. "What's he want?" he demanded. "You ain't gonna give him any money, are you? I tell you, if he's buggin' you, I'll put a welding rod through his lung!" He was peering through the seats, trying in vain to find an opening big enough to squeeze through.

"Goddamn wimp," he added.

I put my arm around the shoulder of the giant chef and sometime designated hitter. "Thanks, but I can handle him."

Then I went looking for some ice—and a place to dump Eddie's roll of film.

The microfilm room of the library turned up just two stories about Tommy Malakis, neither of them major. The first concerned the fire at the Leeward Inn: BAR BLAZE KILLS

ONE. That was the derelict whom Malakis had allowed to sleep in the doorway. His name was Reuben Murtaugh, and he was "a familiar figure in the South of Market neighborhood." It wasn't the first time that Malakis had taken pity on someone and offered him a night's refuge. Police were investigating; arson was a possibility.

Ten months later, there was a three-paragraph story about Malakis's "death." An unidentified assailant had doused in gasoline and set afire a bum in a sleeping bag. The victim was believed to be the former owner of a burned-down bar that had been located a few blocks away. Malakis had been living on the street for some time, according to Michael Sloane, proprietor of a nearby shelter who recognized the charred remains of his sleeping bag. Police had no clue as to the motive behind the attack or the identity of the attacker. An investigation was under way, etc.

Sonia had furnished me with a slim file that was opened when Malakis sought help at the public defender's office. It consisted of a single green interview sheet that indicated no follow-up. The attorney of record was a P.D. by the name of Gordon Kim, who had since moved on to private practice.

And that was it. No pictures of Malakis. No mention of a "treasure." No biographical information. Just the story of a seedy South of Market bar owner who may or may not have torched his business for the insurance money—and who may or may not have ended up the victim of a murder that may or may not have been connected with the fire. Today, the site of the bar was worth several hundred times what it once had been, and was about to be incorporated into a multi-million-dollar complex of hotels and galleries, shops and showrooms. Why Malakis, if he was alive, would have disappeared, only to return for a "treasure" thirteen years later—and why he would seek out Michael Sloane to help him get it—was a mystery.

Tommy Malakis was a faceless nobody—then and now.

Just as Michael had described it, the former site of the Leeward Inn was now an empty corner lot (PARKIT 'N' PAY: TWO DOLLARS A DAY) surrounded by crumbling warehouses and storage yards. To the south and east was the Bay; a rusting cargo ship was visible between the buildings. Heading west you hit the train station. To the north stood the carcass of a brewery, in the midst of conversion to an office building, and above it towered the foundation of the Bay Bridge. The afternoon breeze carried the roar of traffic from on high.

If you look at a map of San Francisco, you'll see that Market Street slashes through the eastern half of the city on a diagonal, breaking the grid and separating north from south. It was done that way for a reason. Some urban planner thought it would be a great idea to create two separate worlds, with Market the demilitarized zone. Above the "Slot" would be banks and businesses and industrialists' mansions; below, the factories and warehouses of the blue-collar world.

It all worked out fine until the factories started closing down and the blue-collar families fled to the suburbs. Suddenly it was open season on South of Market, and the highrises, neon nightclubs, design showrooms, and hotels came flooding over the line. Within a few years there wasn't an acre that hadn't been swallowed up by some new-age developer. As for the winos, they started migrating west, down Mission, Howard, and Bryant Streets: from Third Street to Fifth, from Fifth to Seventh to Eighth. Now they grazed around the Hall of Justice like sick buffalo.

I pushed past the shaky chain-link fence and tried to recreate in my mind the image of a waterfront bar. Nothing materialized. Just paved-over parking lot, with weeds pushing up through asphalt.

I caught the hint of movement from across the street. Something had stirred in the doorway of a weather-beaten warehouse that said STEERS AND CALVES in faded letters. A shadow shifted as if somebody had withdrawn into the building. I crossed over to get a better look.

The door was jammed off its tracks. I squeezed through the opening and stood just inside, waiting for my eyes to adjust to the dimness, and listening.

The place was stuffed with tires, floor to ceiling, row upon row. Maybe they were slated for resurrection as dock bumpers or pieces of a breakwater or whatever else they might be good for. I wondered whether the warehouse had been active in Malakis's day. It seemed older.

Having no desire to be buried under tons of dusty rubber, I started to edge back out. A voice stopped me.

It was almost a whisper, indiscernible as to sex or location. "Is someone there?" it asked. "Help me!"

A flick of fur appeared from behind a tire stack. Then a snout and a lolling tongue. Momentarily a dog poked its head out and looked at me with a stupid grin. It was part shepherd and part something else. I had the creepy feeling that this was the source of the voice. The dog, obviously a stray whose home I had disturbed, whined and withdrew. I went toward it.

The aisle was narrow and I had to turn sideways to squeeze through. Keeping one arm outstretched, I felt my way along. There was an opening up ahead. I reached it, and my hand made contact with a wall. I was in a corner.

Now the animal was back—but behind me this time. And its temperament had changed. It stood thirty feet away, ears back. A growl gurgled up from its stomach. Its eyes were dead-steady pinpricks of light. I backed toward the corner and the dog moved with me. Then the mournful voice spoke again. This time it was clearly a man's.

"Can you chase it away somehow?" he said. "I'm stuck back here."

Peering into the gloom I could just make him out, a tire stack away, pressed against the wall. "I seem to be trapped, too."

"Maybe if we rush them together, we can frighten them off," he said weakly.

My eyes were adjusting. There wasn't one dog blocking the way out; there were three. Their growls merged into a guttural chorus as they edged closer. "Get ready to run," I said to the stranger as a dog flew at me.

I slammed into the nearest stack of tires, trying to shake loose a weapon. It stood like a pillar of cement. I felt the steaming breath of the first dog as it rushed past. Another made straight for my face. I threw up an arm and it knocked me over, jaws locking on my wrist. The man shrieked in the darkness.

I was struggling to my knees when the first dog tackled me from behind. The blow knocked the wind out of me and I couldn't breathe, or see, or cry out. Panic was making me dizzy. I was terrified that I was going to black out. I thrashed about, trying to shake the monsters loose. One was gripping the collar of my jacket, inches from my throat. The other still had my arm. Something tore. *Get up,* my brain was shouting. *On your feet, goddamn it.*

Again I rose from the slippery floor, knees wobbling under the weight of two dogs. My legs buckled. We crashed in a snarling heap into the tire stack and it gave way, beating on us from above, an endless avalanche of black shapes. A dog gave a sickening yelp, but I couldn't cry out because I was choking on dust.

Now I was upright, staggering around, plunging into the tire holes and trying to scramble over a mountain of rotting rubber to the doorway. I was guided by a pale shaft of light. A dog barked in my ear, I stumbled again, grabbed a human arm. Again the man shrieked. We groped for the exit, expecting the beasts to maul us from behind, but we were unpursued as we burst into the blinding whiteness of the day.

I brushed off the grime as best I could while adjusting to the light. The man beside me didn't seem to mind the extra dirt. He was the picture of a derelict, soft and beefy, with a receding hairline and salt-and-pepper beard. Wearing strips of leather that once were a jacket, and a pair of corduroy pants of a color that was no longer identifiable.

"Thank you," he said. "That was . . . very fortuitous thinking." The man seemed barely able to stand, and his words were slurred. He was a cartoon version of a drunk.

"I am very much obliged," he mumbled, shuffling past me. The smell of alcohol was strong. His clothes must have been soaked in it.

"Your home?" I gestured in the direction of the warehouse.

"Wherever. Wherever I am." He was still moving away. "Wherever I happen to be."

"Wait."

He stopped without turning. "I must go now," he said, and started off again.

"How about returning the favor?"

"Don't know what I could do for you."

Damn it, I thought, stop him. Something's not right about this guy. I was certain that he had been watching me from inside the warehouse. Or maybe his voice had something to do with it. The drunkenness was draining from his words.

"Nice way to thank me for saving your life," I said.

The man stopped again, one ear cocked in my direction. He shrugged.

"You from around here or what?" I asked. Stupid question.

No answer.

I came around to face him. He tried to keep his back to me, but ended up moving only a few degrees. "When I'm around."

"Been around a long time?"

He nodded. "Of course. For a good many years." He looked directly at me. "Who wants to know?"

I pointed to the parking lot across the street. "Remember when that was a bar?"

He studied the weed-choked site.

I persisted. "The Leeward Inn. Do you know who used to run it?"

The alcoholic facade vanished. His shoulders rose out of their slump. "Why?"

"I need to find him. I've got something of his that could be valuable. Or somebody I know does."

"You're . . . you're a policeman, aren't you?"

"No, I'm not."

"A private eye?"

I shook my head. "Just helping out a friend. There could be something in it for you, too."

"Enlighten me."

"Forget it." I started to walk away. "You're wasting my time."

"Now wait a minute!" If I left him, we would both come up empty-handed, and he knew it. I kept walking.

"I just might know the man you're looking for," he called out.

"Sorry, I don't believe you."

"I do, I swear."

"Then say his name."

The man stood his ground, chin in the air. He had an obnoxious air of superiority that wasn't typical of a wino. The eyes that were sizing me up were completely lucid. "The name is . . . Clyde."

"Oh, no. Say *his* name."

"Now please . . ."

"Say it or I'm out of here."

"Malakis."

I stopped. "Tell me about him."

"I'm not going to say another word. I know he had a bar over there, like you said. Other than that, nothing." He scraped at the dirt with his boot. "Of course, I might know where to find him, but I'm not in a position to make any promises."

"Okay, Clyde—"

"*Mr.* Clyde."

Only one way to find out what *Mr.* Clyde was up to. "Take me to him."

He pointed a finger at me. "Just remember. I don't get shut out of this little arrangement."

"*If* you really know where Malakis is, you don't."

We started walking. "Who are *you*, anyway?" he asked, stopping suddenly.

"Cassandra Thorpe."

"What kind of a name is that? Are you certain you're not a detective?"

"No. Keep walking."

6

We walked for half an hour—Mr. Clyde wouldn't get into my car—going in circles until he made up his mind to take me to Malakis. I got the story of their meeting in snatches, surrounded by reams of useless information.

Mr. Clyde had come across Malakis in an alley about a month ago. The old man had just been mugged and could barely walk. He claimed to have lost over one hundred dollars, but Mr. Clyde didn't believe it.

Then, just a few days ago, Malakis had begun to speak of his lost bar. He asked Mr. Clyde to find out who now owned the property. That, according to Mr. Clyde, explained his presence in the warehouse—he had ducked in there when he saw me coming. He said nothing about hidden money, but kept probing my reasons for seeking out the old man, and the two of us bobbed and weaved around a subject that neither had any intention of raising. On the surface, we were both exhibiting a groundless fascination with a burned-down bar and a burnt-out bar owner.

We were moving away from the waterfront and into the heart of skid row. Three Vietnamese children clustered around our legs, thrusting out cellophane packages. "Gahlic, mister? Gahlic, lady?" they kept saying tonelessly. Mr. Clyde regarded them like cockroaches. I kept walking. They scampered off.

We passed a man whose face was a twisted mass of scar tissue that looked like a balled-up fist. I almost tripped over the mottled legs of an old woman—at least I think she was old—propped against a garbage can. Refugees in the city of Saint Francis. Finally, Mr. Clyde pulled up at a Folsom Street detox center, a place where addicts and alcoholics could sweat out the agonies of withdrawal in a peaceful environment. A sign hung in a barred window clotted with dirt: YES! WE'RE OPEN.

The buzz of conversation cut off as we drew back the screen door—an odd touch, I thought—and crossed the threshold. At the entrance sat a skinny young man hunched over a card table, studying the want ads. Beyond him were two dozen men, or parts of men: one missing a leg, another an eye, another slumped in a wheelchair. It looked like a Red Cross tent from World War I. The cots were sagging and torn, the rest of the furniture consisting of broken chairs of brightly colored plastic that would have fit perfectly into a House of the Future, circa 1959. The walls sported inspirational messages (LEND A HAND! LET'S PULL TOGETHER!) illustrated by beaming cartoon humans and their cartoon dogs. This was a shelter of last resort.

All eyes followed us as we threaded our way to a cot on which a man slept, a scratchy army-style blanket pulled over his face. A pair of desert boots stood by the bed, each one anchored by a leg of the bed frame.

"I'll wake him up," said Mr. Clyde.

"No, wait." I leaned over the sleeping man and caught a noseful of mothballs and damp wool. "Tommy," I said softly. "Tommy Malakis."

The frail man jerked awake, grabbing at the blanket and pulling it from his face. He looked about sixty, with skin of gray leather, strings of white hair plastered to his scalp, and a nose crisscrossed by blood vessels. He stared at me wildly. "Who are you?"

"Cassandra Thorpe. You're Malakis?"

He looked at me in terror.

I squatted beside the bed. "I can help you if you'll let me."

40

The man looked to Clyde. The fierceness in his bloodshot eyes was demanding an explanation.

I tried again. "Awhile back you wrote a letter to a friend of mine. Now he wants to help. Know what I'm talking about?" about?"

The old man's breath was coming in labored gasps.

"It's okay if you want to keep quiet about this for a while. And if you *don't* want to talk to Michael, that's okay too."

"Leave me the hell alone, will you?" the man on the cot rasped. "I don't need no help." He tore off the blanket and sat on the edge of the bed, trying to free his boots. But the weight of his body prevented him from succeeding. He couldn't seem to figure it out.

"Come on, Tommy. What harm could it do?"

"Get outta here," he growled.

"I can help you get your treasure back."

The word had an electrifying effect on both men. Mr. Clyde exhaled a lungful of air. A calculated risk, but I felt sure he had heard the story. He hadn't pestered me for money up front because he knew there was a bigger reward down the road. As for the man on the bed, he grabbed Mr. Clyde's shirt and shook the bigger man weakly.

"Goddamn it, Clyde," he whined. "Goddamn it. Now you're just walking around town, telling everybody you meet out there—"

"But I haven't told her anything! That's the first she's mentioned it!"

"Then *what* . . ." He lowered his quavering voice. "Listen to me, lady. I ain't Tommy Malakis, and that's a fact."

"What?" said Mr. Clyde.

"Come on, Tommy," I pleaded. "If you want to hide, go ahead and hide, but—"

"I'm telling you the truth!" he blustered, raising his voice enough to be heard by everyone in the room. He paid for the outburst, grabbing his arms and doubling over as shudders ran through him. The man was suffering from an acute case of the alcoholic shakes. A couple of bums meandered over, grateful for the excitement.

"My name is Harry . . . Cremmins," he said in a softer

tone between sobs. His head was still between his knees. "I used to tend bar for Tommy, that's all. We was friends, but I ain't seen him in years. Anyway, he's dead, ain't he? So what's it matter?"

"It matters if you're going around saying you're him. What for? To steal the money?"

"Will you"—Harry Cremmins raised his head and grimaced—"keep it down!" We were drawing a crowd. "Tommy's dead. Whatever's still there . . . it's finders keepers. And I ain't helping nobody else to find it neither! 'Specially not this Mr. Benedict Arnold!" He glared at Mr. Clyde as he spat out the words.

"I can't believe this," said Mr. Clyde. "I really can't believe this."

To keep the visit from coming to an end, or a call to the paramedics, I took Cremmins by the arm and brought him to his feet. He complied meekly, as if he was the patient and I the nurse. I lifted the bed frame and kicked the boots free. Raising my voice just loud enough to make Cremmins uncomfortable, I said, "What if I could help you get at it?"

"Huh?"

"Suppose I can prove that Tommy Malakis really is dead. Then this money is just sitting there waiting for whoever claims it first, just like you say."

Mr. Clyde started in again. "Honest to God, Harry, I didn't say a word to her—"

I cut him off with a look, then turned to Cremmins. "Tell me everything you know about Tommy Malakis, and I'll keep this from getting spread around. That much I can promise. Why don't we walk for a while?"

"That's no deal, that's a *threat*," said Mr. Clyde.

The circle of bums drew tighter. The skinny kid came up and eyed "Harry Cremmins" with suspicion. "There's no arguments in here," he said. "If you gotta make noise, do it in the street."

"Don't worry, we're going," I said to the kid. "We wouldn't dream of messing up your palace."

I handed the boots to Cremmins, and he began putting them on.

The three of us walked, Cremmins in the middle, rambling on about the Leeward Inn. At times he stumbled and had to be propped up.

"I used to work for Malakis. All the time he's bragging 'bout how he's got this money buried in the floor—some stash of old Spanish double-oons, I guess. I don't know. There was this big gold coin he kept nailed up over the bar. That's all I ever saw. Used to point it out to the customer. 'That's just one of them,' he'd say. 'I got a hunnerd more.' He'd shine that sucker till you could see yourself in it."

That didn't sound like gold. "Were they his? Did he say where they came from?"

"Used to be a boardinghouse, he said. Some old sea captain lived there. Kept his money in gold. Supposed to be a long time ago, 'fore the quake. Long as I remember, the place was a bar. Tommy's bar."

"And what happened to Tommy's bar?"

"Only know what I heard. I was gone when the place got torched." He looked at me in alarm. "I was! Long gone!"

Some friend. "But you know Malakis never got his treasure, don't you?"

"Well, I heard he was on the street. You don't stay on the street if you're loaded down with gold double-oons, now do you?" He cleared his throat violently and spat into the gutter.

"But what makes you think the treasure's still there?"

"'Cause nobody's found it, have they? 'Sides, ain't nobody but me believed him when he talked about it anyhow."

"Have you looked?"

"Well, a course I've looked, lady. It's just gonna take some time to find, that's all. Got to get me a shovel and whatnot."

"But it's been thirteen years. How come you're looking now?"

Cremmins stopped in a doorway and picked up an open bottle of white port, draining two or three drops into his mouth. Two punk rockers passed by, clad in studded leather and chains. They snickered at the bum.

"Fucking punks," Cremmins said, tossing the bottle away.

It smashed against the door. "None a that shit up north. Clean up there." He muttered something before picking up the thread. "Just got into town. Heard he was dead. It ain't stealing when he's dead."

"Do you know how Malakis died?"

"Ain't heard that, I guess. What happen, he got beat up or something, right, Clyde?"

Mr. Clyde shrugged. "The first I ever heard of Tommy Malakis was from you, Harry. When you told me that *you* were him. Then from Miss Thorpe here." He turned to me. "Whom did you say you work for?"

Cremmins interrupted my answer. "Hey, lady, you got forty-seven cents? That's all I need for a bowl a soup, and they'll be serving it up in a few minutes. I got to get cleaned up."

I handed him a dollar. "By the way," I said, "did anybody ever offer to buy the bar while you worked there?"

Cremmins studied the dollar bill. "No. Never heard nothing 'bout that. Like I said, nobody believed the story."

"Except you."

He grabbed the dollar and shoved it into his pocket. Bitterness over his own inertia had hardened him into a fulltime bum. He seemed more interested in the "treasure" as a story, something to dream about between drinks, than as a source of wealth.

"Harry," I said, "we're going to get you a nicer place to sleep tonight than that pit over on Folsom. How does that sound?"

"I can't . . . can't do no more right now. I'm fine where I am." The walk had tired him out. "Gotta get dinner."

"They have food, too." I took an arm and moved him along. Mr. Clyde started to follow.

"Not you," I said. "This is private."

Mr. Clyde's belly drooped. "We had an agreement—"

"You'll hear from me. Take this." I tore off a piece of paper and wrote down the number of Shade's Bail Bonds. In my six months as an investigator, I hadn't bothered to have business cards printed up. "Now go on," I said. "I'll call you."

He snatched the scrap away from me and took off down the street in a huff. "No, *you* will hear from *me*," he called out. "And soon!"

I pulled Cremmins in the opposite direction. He stumbled after me, muttering to himself. We were headed for The Wayside. Only Michael Sloane could tell me if this was Tommy Malakis.

The sky was going gray; most of the neighborhood was gathering in the soup kitchens. The few people still on the street all seemed to have some destination in mind. Except for one man. He stood across the street behind a chain-link fence surrounding another two-dollar parking lot. He had a pale complexion and stark white hair tortured into a crew cut that stuck straight up from his head. He looked to be almost six and a half feet tall. His eyes were paler than his skin, almost colorless, and he was staring at me.

The man didn't move, didn't look away. Cremmins and I stood at the curb. We had been about to cross the street.

I changed my mind, dragging Cremmins off in another direction. He complained, of course, but I ignored him, and just kept both of us moving. Fast.

7

The Wayside was packed. The "guests" sat shoulder to shoulder on benches, devouring the contents of their plastic trays: turkey roll in gravy, green peas, brown 'n' serve rolls, and a half-pint carton of milk. I expected Jimmy Cagney to leap onto a table at any minute and start knocking things around.

Cremmins hovered outside the dining room, intimidated by the boisterous crowd. "There ain't no room in there," he said over the noise. "Lemme go away by myself!" He kept rubbing his mouth, contorting his features horribly. The man was dying of thirst.

I spotted Michael toward the back. He was yelling at a black man in his twenties, dressed in an expensive-looking suede jacket and dark slacks. Michael shoved at him as he spoke, but the man, who was six inches taller, didn't strike back. He stood his ground, palms upright, trying to explain. Finally Michael spun him around and marched him toward the door. As they approached, I could hear Michael say, "Just get the hell out of my place! I don't want to see your face, hear me?"

"Oh, man, what is this shit?" the black man kept saying as Michael shoved him toward us. "This is jive, man."

"I'll jive your ass, punk, if I see it around here again! Hear that? Tell your boss, too. The Wayside is out of bounds for you scum!"

"Watch it, man." The intruder was backing away now. "Watch for it."

"Don't threaten me, asshole." With one last push Michael propelled the man through the door. Michael's reaction was understandable. When you're a former heroin addict, you're not likely to be well-disposed toward dope dealers on your turf.

"Bravo, cowboy," I said when he turned back to the room.

Michael adjusted his rolled-up sleeves. "These punks think they can come in here and deal drugs behind my back. What do they take me for, anyway?"

"Who's going to buy from them? Most of your guests can't raise the price of a bottle."

"They got ways they can pay. As lookouts, as spitters . . . but what are you doing here?"

"I brought somebody over." I pulled Cremmins toward me.

"Who's he?" Michael asked.

"Just somebody who would like something to eat," I said.

Michael looked Cremmins over with disapproval. "He doesn't look so good."

I waited for some sign of recognition between the two. Finally I said, "Michael—Harry Cremmins. Harry—Michael Sloane."

Cremmins ignored the introduction. He was starting to get the shakes again.

"Can I speak to you for a moment?" I asked Michael. He shrugged, but followed me to a corner while Cremmins leaned against a wall and fought off his hallucinations. "Well," I said. "Is it him?"

"Who?"

"*Malakis*, damn it! Why do you think I brought him here?"

Michael took a good look at Cremmins. "No, it's not," he finally said.

"Have you ever met him?"

"Can't say that I have."

47

"So much for brilliant theories."

"What?"

"Nothing."

"Where did you find him?" Michael asked.

"In a drunken stupor at the detox center." Maybe Cremmins is who he says he is. Now all of a sudden two "friends" just happen to be looking for the same "treasure" at the same time. Are they searching together, or is it a race? *Tell no one,* Malakis's note had read.

"Well, thanks a lot," Michael said. "This is no halfway house. Look at him, the guy can barely stand up, he ought to be in a hospital."

"These are special circumstances. He may lead us to Malakis."

"How's he going to do that? He can't even lead himself to the toilet."

"Will you just give him a bed for a few nights? I don't want to lose him."

"I don't see *you* inviting him home. Why me?"

"Because you're the one who hatched this lamebrained scheme in the first place!" My temper was rising. "Did I come to you and say, 'Please, Michael, give me an idiotic case to work on so I can stick around this lovely neighborhood awhile longer'? This is some great hospitality!"

Michael sighed, then returned to Cremmins, taking the pale, shaking man by the arm. "Come on," he said, "let's get you cleaned up."

"God, I need a drink!" Cremmins wailed.

"Good morning law offices. One moment please, I'll see if he's in. Good morning law offices. Yes, sir. One moment please. Good morning law offices. I'll give you his secretary. One moment. Good morning . . ."

The phone kept ringing with little electronic burps. The receptionist had a buttery voice that never varied in tone or volume. Her "good morning law offices" routines were punctuated by nimble button pushing on a console that she never looked at. She was cruising on autopilot.

I was engulfed in a leather couch, studying the engravings

on the wall—drawings from Dickens's time, caricatures of barristers and judges arguing in grotesque poses. The firm specialized in personal injury cases, the kind where the winning attorney walks away with half of a three-million-dollar settlement to compensate for somebody's broken fibula. The building was a converted warehouse on Pacific Avenue, above the Financial District, in an area where medium-rise office buildings were pushing out the furniture showrooms and sending them South of Market. I was waiting to see Gordon Kim, the name on the single sheet of paper that constituted the public defender's file on Tommy Malakis.

A tall secretary in spiked heels and jangling bracelets led the way to Kim's office. It had a parquet floor with a roughly woven white rug in the center. One wall was exposed brick, restored from earlier days. A complete skeleton hung from a hook in the corner; no doubt it was used by the lawyers to tell juries about their clients' concussions or contusions or occlusions, or whatever.

Gordon Kim was Chinese, about forty, dressed in a three-piece suit creased in all the right places. He looked as if he got a haircut every three days.

"So you're with the P.D.'s, huh? I was sooo happy to get out of there. This place is like another world. I was a P.D. for five years, can you believe it? How long for you?"

"Nine."

"Yeah, you're ready for a change."

"Excuse me?"

Kim had returned to his desk. I sat in one of his client chairs, an antique reproduction. "Okay," he said. "Here's the program. You'll find they don't put a big premium on criminal trial experience around here. I know, I was surprised too. And nine years—they might think you're some kind of bureaucrat. But if you make it, you can expect sixty, maybe sixty-five a year. And two years' partnership credit."

"I quit the P.D.'s a year ago."

"Well, that's all right, a year's not too long—"

"I'm not looking for a job."

Kim seemed to notice me for the first time. "You're not?"

"Actually, I'm doing a little investigative work. It's about Tommy Malakis."

"Malakis . . . Malakis. Do I know him?"

I handed him the green sheet.

Kim studied it. He still wasn't sure whether to believe me. Finally he said, "Yeah, now I remember . . . somebody died in that fire, right?"

"That's the one."

He did a drum fill on the desktop with his Cross pen. "Yeah . . . that guy was a nut." He gave out a derisive laugh. "But then so was everybody, right? I had this client once—"

"Can you tell me about Malakis?"

"Okay, okay," he said, taken aback by my refusal to shoot the breeze about the good old days. "He seemed real paranoid, said somebody was after him. I thought he meant the cops, you know, because he was trying to collect on the insurance, but they were claiming that he had set the fire."

"*Who* was after him?"

"I could never get him to say. I think it was all in his mind. You know, a guy loses everything and the insurance company won't pay off. So he goes around saying that somebody's trying to kill him, take his bar away. It's his way of protecting himself, I guess."

"Apparently it didn't work."

"What do you mean?"

His ignorance seemed sincere. "Somebody *did* get to him," I said. "They found his body in Wino Park not long after that."

The gold pen stopped drumming.

"You'd think the news would have gotten back somehow," I said.

"You realize how many cases I was handling back then? Three, four felony trials on calendar every Monday morning—you know how it is. Listen, this Malakis guy came in to see me twice, said he was being chased by someone, and was gone, zap. The D.A. didn't have enough to take it to trial, so the whole thing got dropped. He beat the rap, the insurance company kept its money, and that was the last I heard of him."

"He didn't want a lawyer to help him go after the insurance money?"

"If he did, he never asked me about it."

"He said someone was trying to take his bar away? What did he mean?"

"I thought he meant somebody wanted to buy it. Said he'd had some offers. Of course it became moot after the place burned down. There was nothing left to buy."

"Can you remember who made those offers? Please think hard—it could be important."

Kim shook his head. "He never said."

It was the first concrete evidence that somebody might have been interested in buying the bar. If I could only find out who. . . . "Ever hear of a man named Harry Cremmins?"

"Is that the guy who was after him?"

"I'm not sure. How about Reuben Murtaugh? He was killed in the bar fire."

Kim shrugged. "I'm not being much help to you, am I?"

The scene was an easy one to picture. Tommy Malakis, possibly terrified for his life, comes to the public defender's office for help, and all he gets is an initial interview and the brush-off. The insurance company is coming down on his head, and the D.A. is threatening to put him in jail. Then, when he turns up dead, nobody bothers to remember that he had predicted it—no follow-up, no questions asked. Bring on the next batch of cases.

I got up to leave. "Did he say anything to you about a 'treasure'?"

"Treasure? I don't understand."

"Just the word. Did he ever use it?"

"He was babbling about lots of things, like I said. I was in the middle of a rape-kidnap trial with a G.B.I., and to tell you the truth, I didn't pay a whole lot of attention to him after that."

"It seems nobody did." I didn't tell him that Malakis was supposed to be alive after all. It wouldn't have meant anything to him.

The skeleton leered at me from the corner. Come work for

us, it seemed to say. Forget about bums and winos and psychos and people who stink. This is where the money is. And
it's a lot cleaner, too.

"Whoa, wait a minute," said Kim. I had reached the door.
"What's this all mean? We never took the case, so if somebody's trying to make trouble about it, there's no compe-
tency of counsel issue here at all."

"Don't worry. If it's something that's coming back to haunt
you, I'll let you know."

He seemed perplexed, but shook it off. "Hey, you sure
you're not looking for work in the private sector? I've helped
lots of P.D.s escape from the clutches of civil service."

"I'll let you know that, too."

I brushed past a potted palm and let myself out. I needed
air.

8

After my journey to the world of designer lawyering, South of Market seemed like home. I was troubled by a revulsion for Gordon Kim's ferns and varnished wood surfaces that I could neither explain nor shake off. Was this what Santa Rosa would be like? Quiet, comfortable, secure—and somehow alien? There was an openness to the squalor of skid row. Every day the same familiar faces were spread out on the pavement, huddled in the doorways, lined up at the shelters. I *knew* these people.

Crossing the wide street to my office, I passed the shopping-cart man. He wore a slick yellow raincoat rain or shine, and pushed a cart around all day overflowing with his own treasures—coat hangers, crushed aluminum cans, pieces of masonry, whatever happened to look tempting at the moment. A shiny hubcap was wired to the front of the cart. He moved with an extraordinary sense of purpose, a man doggedly pursuing his chosen career. He was eminently sane. Was Tommy Malakis? What if his "treasure" was as valuable as the shopping-cart man's? Maybe he kept a rusty strongbox in the cellar, filled with brightly colored bits of cloth, or picture postcards of Sutro Baths and expired bus transfers. Maybe the gold coin was a shiny piece of brass that came out of a vending machine at the Cliff House, embossed with his name. I made a mental note to check the hospitals—"quietly," of course.

Elroy was slumped in front of my building in the alley, grinning the enormous grin that signaled his boarding the Night Train Express early. "You knooow what I want, sweetie," he gargled.

"I hope it's not a kiss. 'Cause you're not going to get one." He was blocking the entrance to the stairwell. I tried to squeeze by.

"I've been waiting, sweetie," he toothed. "Gotta present for you, aaargh."

"I don't really need anything right now, Elroy, although it's a nice—" I was looking at a gun, a greasy .22-caliber pistol of the Saturday-night-special variety. It was my clients' weapon of choice, back at the P.D.'s. Elroy was pointing it at me.

I froze, trying to settle on something to say. Elroy just sat there one step below, half turned with the gun pointed straight at the bridge of my nose. His mouth stretched back to reveal gray, rotted gums. It was a smile.

"Uh . . . what's that?" I managed. An extremely intelligent comment.

"A gun," he said, impatient over my ignorance. "Found it in a alley, aar. It's for you. You be needing it, I'm sure." He shoved the weapon at me, barrel first.

I pushed it away, perhaps a little too violently. "Don't need a gun, Elroy." Then I thought again. He hadn't been in jail for three weeks, and he was due.

"Uh, on second thought, I'll take it. You never know."

"No, aaah, you never *ever* know," he said, handing over the weapon. It felt like a toy. I wondered whether it was loaded.

"Now can I have a dollar?"

I gave him some money; he "aarghed" and went away, thanking me profusely and promising to pay me back soon.

Get rid of the thing fast. That was my first thought. I had never used a gun and wasn't about to learn how. I didn't even have a license to operate as an investigator, much less a permit to carry a weapon, and in all likelihood I would shoot off my foot. So I stuffed it in my purse and tried to ease past the doorway of Shade's Bail Bonds without being noticed.

"Cass, is that you?" Adrian called out. "There's messages in here."

Pushing the gun deeper into my purse, I stepped into the bail bonds office. Two desks, two filing cabinets, and a typing table occupied every last inch of space. The standing joke was that Art Shade had hired a five-foot-tall receptionist because no one larger could fit in his office. Adrian was squeezed into the desk behind the door. She had a narrow view of the television that sat atop one of the file cabinets. Left on twenty-four hours a day, it drowned out the incessant buzzing of the neon BAIL BONDS sign that hung in the window. On the other desk lay a dirty white poodle, buried in a heap of blankets, transfixed by the television show. The animal was completely blind, but it seemed to derive comfort from the sound of the TV. Maybe it liked the drone of the organ on the soaps.

"This is for you." Adrian handed me a manila envelope. Inside were three police reports and a handwritten note: CASS, THIS IS ALL I COULD FIND. HAVE YOU GOT MY FILM? EDDIE.

"Somebody keeps calling but won't leave a message," Adrian said. "A man. Then there's these." She handed over two pink slips, both from Sonia. "Not a lot of business these days, huh."

Adrian was watching TV as she spoke, even though she never looked at the screen. She had the rare gift of giving complete attention to two things at once: soap operas and the rest of the world. She didn't miss an episode of "The Edge of Night" between its debut in 1956 and the day it was taken off the air almost thirty years later.

"Thanks, Adrian. I'll see you later." My purse almost slipped off my shoulder as I maneuvered in the tiny room, but I managed to prevent the gun from falling out. I looked over the contents of the manila envelope while climbing the stairs. The smell of urine was winning out over the disinfectant that day.

The first police report had nothing to do with the Malakis case. It concerned Eddie's car accident—the one for which I still had the pictures. CASS, I NEED HELP ON THIS!!! Eddie had written, triple-underlined. I put the report on the bottom of the stack.

Next was the police report on Reuben Murtaugh, the man who died in the bar fire. Like the paper said, he was a drifter whom Malakis had allowed to sleep on the premises. Somebody named Gerald Geraghty had made the positive I.D.; police said Geraghty and Murtaugh were "inseparable." The relationship apparently dated back to county jail—in fact they had returned there together several times. More than once Murtaugh had picked a fight with a bigger man, then Geraghty had beaten the guy to a pulp. There was no visible connection between Murtaugh and Malakis, other than the bar owner's tolerance of bums in doorways.

The report on Tommy Malakis was even less revealing. There was Michael Sloane's name, along with comments from others in the neighborhood who had seen Malakis in the park the previous three or four nights. A few had drunk in his bar once or twice, but nobody knew him well, so there was no mention of hidden money, attempts to buy the place before it burned down, or a mysterious pursuer. The only hard evidence was a few shreds of Michael's Smokey the Bear sleeping bag and a tentative identification of human remains. In short, the perfect disappearing act for someone who wanted to get away, forever.

So what? If he now wanted to come back and dig up an old parking lot by himself, why not let him? Despite his letter to Michael, he had good reason to go it alone. For one thing, there was Harry Cremmins, just waiting for the right opportunity to go treasure hunting himself. Malakis probably was hiding in the shadows, waiting to see what Cremmins would do. For all I knew he was watching me, too. Well, I thought, let him watch. And let him stay safe. I would remain on the case for two more weeks, to keep Michael happy, but if I came up empty-handed at the end of that time—so much the better.

I placed the gun in the top drawer of the file cabinet and slammed it shut.

"Miss Thorpe!" I jumped as if I had been caught with an Uzi.

There in the doorway stood Sherman Tuttle, briefcase and all. He had on plaid pants and a plaid jacket, but they were different plaids. He slipped into the office and shut the door. "Were you seen coming in?" he whispered. "Who was that kimmie you were talking to?"

"I wasn't aware that I was reporting to you."

"Yibe, I know how you must feel. I am sorry." He looked sad, and I felt a spark of guilt for my nasty tone. "That is really why I am here." Tuttle took a seat, propped the brief-case on his knees, adjusted his taped-up glasses, and began fiddling with the combination. The trembling in his hands had worsened. "I have come to the conclusion that you are not a spy."

"That's comforting. I was getting worried."

"This is not a time for jokes, Miss Thorpe." The briefcase popped open, and he placed on the desk a dirty white legal-sized envelope, sealed with fingerprinted Scotch tape.

"You should be aware," he said, tapping the envelope, "that you are the only person I can trust. I acted too hastily when I saw you with Michael Sloane. I understand now that you were merely undertaking the investigation on my be-half."

"You seem to know a lot about *my* movements. Who's the spy here, anyway?"

"Never mind that. Just be aware that I am hiring you again. I need your help very badly. Please keep this enve-lope in your possession in a *very safe place*, as it is of great importance to me. I will be back for it as soon as I can. In the meantime, I expect you will be continuing on the case. You must act fast. Sloane's plans are moving ahead. Re-member about the web."

"That's enough." Time to stop babying him. I pushed the envelope away. "Listen to me, Mr. Tuttle. I am *not* a private investigator. I never have been one, and never intend to be one. I don't have a license. I'm lousy at it. I don't even like it. Do you understand? You can't hire me."

Tuttle put on his uncomprehending stare, making an O with his lips. Slowly, amazingly, comprehension dawned.

57

"You are *not* an investigator."

"That's right."

"Never have been."

"Uh-huh."

"I see." He looked at the briefcase as if it contained the answer to this conundrum. I thought he was going to start talking to it. At last he put an elbow on the desk, cocked his head, and leaned toward me. "Then what are you?"

"I am a lawyer."

"Ah." He thought about that one. Spirits rose and he was back in the briefcase, pulling out a thick and tattered Pee-Chee folder and slapping it on the desk. "Then I would like to secure your services. We will adopt a new strategy. I will sue Michael Sloane, and you will be my attorney. The charges are criminal larceny, conspiracy, malicious intent, madge-house in slugging nook, and . . . wait, I have depositions, sworn statements . . . let me just find my Penal Code—"

"Stop!" So much for honesty. "I, uh, might have given you the wrong impression. You see, I'm not really a lawyer. I'm just, uh . . . doing some investigative work now, but—"

"Then you are hired again," Tuttle said triumphantly. "I am glad that you have changed your mind. Here." He held out the dirty white envelope. I took it, if only to make him withdraw his arm. The outline of a key could be felt through the paper. Tuttle dropped his voice to a whisper. "I will give you a clue," he said. "I suspect some kind of a coup."

In place of amusement I felt only annoyance. When you've lost your sense of humor, they used to say at the P.D.'s, you're dead. I didn't care. All I knew was that Tuttle wasn't going to be as easy to shake as Michael had suggested. Humor him, Cass, tell him you've looked into the matter, he'll go away. Fat chance.

"I must go now." The briefcase snapped shut and Tuttle shot up from the chair. "I will be in touch."

I softened my attitude. "Sherman, I'm trying to explain something here. . . . It doesn't matter *what* I am; I can't take the case. You're just going to have to find somebody else."

He smiled. "Underst." It was the smugness of borderline insanity: indisputable, impenetrable. Looking both ways into the stairwell, he turned back to face me. "And I will come near to you to judgment, and I will be a swift witness against the sorcerers," he said. "You really should do something about the smell on these stairs." Then he glided out.

I stared at the bare walls and furnishings: a desk, two chairs, a wooden file cabinet painted olive drab and stuffed with invoices from a defunct import-export company, and a stack of Chinese eight-track tapes piled in a corner halfway to the ceiling. The desk had been bare when I moved in, except for an empty bottle of Night Train Express at the back of a drawer. I was using it as a vase for the wilted flowers that Elroy brought me from time to time. Today they looked more like weeds. This was the office of Cassandra Thorpe Investigations.

The feeling of familiarity had vanished. South of Market seemed no less foreign than Gordon Kim's slick designer life. Something was missing from both worlds. I turned to the window in frustration, still holding the grimy envelope with THORP scrawled in ocher felt pen. The smokestack on Potrero Hill was spewing a black vapor that blended with the darkening sky. Clouds were racing overhead, scraps of summer fog off the Bay. The scrawny dog in the backyard below had his head in a hole. Down in the alley, the shopping-cart man rattled by, and from somewhere out of sight a black man was crying out, "I'm comin' on! I'm comin' on! I told you I was comin' on! Better look out 'cause I'll be there soon!"

I wanted out of there so bad.

9

Early morning, South of Market. The shady side of
the street was still bitter cold, and the sunny side wasn't
much warmer. The fog had retreated to the avenues, leaving
a thick soaking of dew. The Filipinos and Chinese who
worked in the sweatshops and warehouses were waiting outside for their supervisors to come take the padlocks off the
doors. Men in tight T-shirts and leather pants were filing out
of the S&M bathhouses, unmarked buildings with boarded-
over windows that closed when the sun came up. Two dozen
bums were huddled in front of one of the "reception cen-
ters," or detox clinics, which kicked them out at six o'clock
every morning for cleanup and let them back in at eight. In a
park a bum was stirring from a bed of newspaper and cardboard, his body stiff from the night air. A couple of Vietnamese children passed on their way to school. Down the
block a man was slumped against a wall, so motionless he
could very well be dead. Above him was a billboard pictur-
ing an elegant black woman looking over her shoulder seduc-
tively and saying, "I assume you drink Martell."

Sonia had finally convinced me to take a couple of small
jobs for her during the time I would be staying in the city for
Michael. One of her clients had been caught with a carful of
speakers, turntables, and video recorders, and insisted that

he was only borrowing the vehicle from a "cousin." He knew nothing about the stereo emporium in the trunk, of course. I was standing in front of the address he had given as that of the car's owner. It was nothing but a shack and a yard ridden with trash, protected by chain-link and barbed wire. Behind it the rusting body of a Thunderbird squatted on cinder blocks. A searchlight, corroded by years of exposure, was mounted on an open trailer. Across the back of the light was stenciled CREEDY'S SPECTACULARS, with a phone number. An old man in overalls was polishing the glass with Windex, cigarette dangling from his mouth.

"Morning, miss!" he said, shaking out the towel. "Need a light?"

"I don't smoke."

He chuckled. "I mean this." He slapped the searchlight. "For rent any time you need it. Weddings, parties, premieres. Got its own generator, so it's portable. This light has been around."

"Do you own a 'seventy-three Pinto? Bright red?"

"No, I do not." He resumed his polishing. "But I've got this T-Bird here if you're interested. They're my specialty, you know. Must have fixed up twenty of 'em by now. What a car."

I agreed, but said I had no use for a Thunderbird or a searchlight just then. What I really wanted was a six-unit apartment building standing on this property, to corroborate the lame story of Sonia's client. I headed back to the office to disappoint her.

The *San Francisco Herald* sums up the news of the day at the top of page 1, so it can be seen through the clear plastic of the honor box. I perused it while waiting for the light to change. At first one of the items didn't register. I had to read it twice. It said, "Rumors of murder and buried money surround a bar that burned down in the South of Market area 13 years ago. Page 4."

My hands were shaking badly, so it took a long time to fish a quarter out of my purse and slip it into the coin slot. It fell to the sidewalk on the first try. Finally I had the newspaper open before me. PARKING LOT MAY HIDE FORTUNE, MURDER MYSTERY, it said. By Phillip Harrington, Jr.

And there it all was: the history of Malakis's bar, his boasting about the treasure, his violent death on a cold night in Wino Park. The story focused on Harry Cremmins, portraying him as a bum with dreams of unearthing a dead man's fortune. There was no mention that Cremmins had tried to pass himself off as Malakis.

The capper came further down in the piece. "But Tommy Malakis may not be dead after all," it said. "At least one person suspects that he has returned to town to reclaim his property." And who was the source for this earthshaking news? "According to private detective Cassandra Thorpe, who is looking into the Malakis case . . ."

On my way over to the offices of the *Herald* I tried to think—to the extent I could think at all—how the story was broken. No reporter had contacted me. Yet I was quoted throughout. It had to be Michael's doing, meaning he had altered his tactics and perhaps no longer even needed my services. But why would he dump it all on me? To deceive the developers? In a way it didn't matter. Somebody had gone public with the Malakis story, and that changed everything. A million people knew about it now.

My old public defender's card got me past the guard at the newspaper office, and somebody directed me through the obstacle course of desks to Phillip Harrington's work area. Even from across the room I recognized him as "Mr. Clyde." The bum who had listened as Harry Cremmins spilled what he knew about Tommy Malakis. Who knew everything that I did, if not more. Perched on the desk beside him, sipping coffee from a Styrofoam cup and reading the racing form, was my ex-husband, Eddie.

Eddie saw me first. He closed the newspaper and creased it neatly. "Yo, how's it going? Some story, wasn't it? Man, it's got everything—money, murder, sex. No, I guess no sex. But wouldn't it make like a great flick? Let me know if you're interested. I know who to see."

I shoved Eddie aside and stood before Phillip Harrington,

Jr. He was leaning back, hands behind his head, copious belly straining the buttons of his frayed tattersall shirt. He was grinning.

"I see you got a well-paying job, Mr. Clyde." My voice sounded unnaturally shrill.

"Okay, you're probably a bit upset—"

"Upset!"

"Now just hold on. Normally I would have identified myself right away, but this was a case of rather special circumstances, I'm sure you'll agree. I was undercover, doing a piece on what it's like to live on the street. A five-part series. Eating with the bums, drinking with them, sleeping with them . . . well, you hear what I'm saying. I couldn't possibly tell you the truth. It was a judgment call."

"So you took advantage of me, and Cremmins, and maybe Malakis too—"

"Now what would you have done? I met somebody who claimed he was a dead man and had a *buried treasure* concealed in a parking lot! And then you showed up, asking about the same man and the same bar. . . ." He clicked his tongue. "A *great* story."

"Yeah, what a coincidence. And your pal here?"

Eddie started to open his mouth, but Harrington spoke first. "Eddie and I happen to be friends from—"

"Do you know what you are, Harrington?"

"I am a reporter. Reporters report. It's my job."

"You are slime with worms."

Harrington threw up his hands. "So be that way. But your attitude seems rather pointless. Really, when I think about it, you ought to thank me. You're looking for Malakis, and I got the story out."

The anger was welling up behind my eyes. Screw control, I thought. I'd like to slit this guy's belly with a letter opener. "If he's not dead," I managed to say, "he will be soon."

I grabbed Eddie by the arm. "Hey, watch the jacket," he said, as I dragged him away.

"This happens to be a great opportunity for you," said Harrington to my back. "We can collaborate, you know.

You guarantee an exclusive, and I'll hold back from now on. . . ."

I pushed my ex-husband through the swinging doors—he nearly lost a hand in the process—and out to the street. "'Yeah,'" I mocked. "'Eddie and I happen to be friends.'"

Eddie shrugged, smoothing out the lapels on his raw silk blazer. "So what do you want from me? Sure I knew Phil at the paper. He was at the cop station when I was getting those reports. We got to talking. What could I do? He like knew about this Malakis guy already. And when he saw what *I* was after, he wouldn't get off my back till I told him what was going on. And besides, I swore him to secrecy, the bastard—"

I was going for the lapels again when the police car pulled up. The driver leaned across and rolled down the window. "Come over here," he said.

"Oh great," Eddie said. "Now look what you've done. You've made a scene, and the cops are gonna bust me, and you'll have to bail me out. . . ." He slapped me away and swaggered over to the police car.

The cop, a beefy man with one of those stupid little cop mustaches, got out and held the back door open. Eddie climbed in as if it was a chauffeured limousine. "Judge wants to see you about a fender bender," the cop said. "Seems you've got a habit of not showing up in court."

I knew the cop. It was Officer Martin Kessler, speaking in the same sneering tone he had used a couple of years ago when he promised to frame me for a drug bust. "Don't be surprised to find me at your door some night," he had said. I had just finished tearing him to pieces on the witness stand. His threat had been preceded by a dinner invitation.

Don't recognize me, I thought fiercely. *I'm not in the mood. I just want to—*

"Miss Thorpe! What are *you* doing here?" Kessler was acting happy to see me. "You representing your boy in this thing?"

"That's none of your business."

"Looks like he's been moonlighting as an ambulance chaser. Kind of like a lawyer, huh? Guess his paper won't be too happy to hear about it."

"In case you're interested, I'm not working for the paper anymore," Eddie called out from the car.

"Why don't you just shut up?" Kessler snapped. Then to me, "Said he was a reporter on the accident report."

Kessler started to get in the car, then turned back to me. "But how about you? I heard *you* changed jobs too."

"I left the P.D.'s. You knew that."

"Yeah, right. Bad break. Hell of a screw-up there. And you're an investigator now, right?"

"Not really."

"Not really? Oh, I get it, a secret agent. Gee, you carrying a gun? Got a microphone hidden in your Tampax?"

Eddie broke in. "Hey, that's kinda uncalled for—"

"I said shut up, punk," Kessler snarled. Eddie slumped down in the seat. The cop turned back to me and smiled sweetly. "Do tell."

"If you're going to arrest me, too, Kessler, do it. Otherwise leave me alone."

"There's no need to be hostile, honey. I'm just asking after your welfare. Saw your name in the paper and wanted to talk to a celebrity." Kessler pointed to a news vendor in front of the building. "Unless that was some other Cassandra Thorpe."

I didn't respond.

"Didn't think so. So I guess you got a license and everything, huh? That's really great, I mean it."

"It's not a business." Why doesn't he go away?

"Oh, I see. 'Cause I would just hate to think you were running afoul of the law these days. Like with no license, and maybe a bad old firearm without a permit or something."

I started to blurt out some choice responses but shut myself up in time. Control, damn it. Don't let him get to you.

Fuck off, Marty, I thought, and I felt better.

Kessler gave me his cute tough-guy look, got in the car, and pulled away. I stood on the sidewalk beside the stack of a hundred papers containing the Malakis story, trying to keep my muscles from shaking.

"Hey, Cass!" Eddie yelled from the receding police car. "Bail me outta here!"

10

To escape the torrent of phone calls and further harassment from officers of the law—and to buy some time before I'd have to face Michael—I took refuge in the Hall of Records. The idea was to do some checking up on the history of 100 Barron Street, former location of the Leeward Inn. Malakis said there used to be a boardinghouse on the spot. If an "old sea captain" really did live on the premises, it most likely would have been before 1906, the year South of Market was devastated by the big earthquake and fire.

Finding a mention of Malakis's ownership of the bar was easy enough. The county sales ledgers showed that Thomas and Leona Malakis acquired it in 1949. I wondered what had happened to Leona. The sellers were listed as Philip and Federico d'Angeli. According to the deed in the recorder's office, the d'Angeli Brothers operated a seafood warehouse there all the way back to 1914. There didn't seem to be any records reaching beyond that.

A circle of desks was surrounded by shelves built to hold huge record books, made dark and brittle by age. Clerks from the various title companies sat here. Today only one was around.

The woman was barely twenty-one, sporting a modified

punk hairdo and a hot pink miniskirt with black go-go boots. The same dress was stuffed in the back of my closet, but I hadn't had the guts to wear it for eighteen years. She was straining to shove an oversized records book onto a shelf three feet above her head.

"Let me do it," I said, taking the volume from her and replacing it in the bookcase.

"Oh Christ, thank you," she gasped. Her attempts to smooth out the tufts of hair were having no visible effect. "Someday I'll be killed by one of these goddamn books. Industrial accidents are the worst."

My hands were coated with dust. "I can't seem to find any property records going back further than 1914."

"Um, there aren't any—at least ones that were kept by the city," she said. "They didn't care about stuff like that back then."

"I would have thought the earthquake would be the cutoff date."

"Christ, no. The bureaucracy was a bigger disaster than the quake. You've got to understand, this attention to detail, they didn't have it back then."

"Where can I find older records?"

She handed me another giant book, and led the way to its place on the shelf. "The private title companies. Of course, we're the only ones who really go that far. Some of our stuff goes back to 1850."

"Who's 'we'?" The book almost slipped from my grasp as I shoved it into place.

"The company I work for—Tillits and Whelan. That's my little desk, right over there. We've got the best records of anyone."

I handed her a scrap of paper with the assessment block and lot number of the Leeward Inn. "What was this before 1914?"

The girl shook her head. "Most of that was just docks and water and empty space, but I can check."

She disappeared down another aisle. I looked over the current ownership records of the assessment block. Parchment and chisel-points had given way to microfiche. The labored flourishes of the old scribes were long gone. And there was a numbing monotony of content now as well: every lot on the block was owned by Sunrise Development. Most of the adjacent property had also been gobbled up, giving the developers nearly three blocks of uninterrupted, prime real estate with a Bay view. The acquisition dates were spread throughout the years, but the purchase of Malakis's property—which had been sold off by the county— was one of the first. The people behind Sunrise Development were thinking many moves ahead.

The girl returned, bearing a single note card. "Don't know why you'd care," she said, consulting her scribblings, "but this whole part of Barron Street was open space before the quake. The Dan-jellys—that how you pronounce it?—built a warehouse in 1907. Like I said, before that, nothing. All that's landfill, most of Yerba Buena Cove was underwater till 1850 or so."

She handed me the note card. "Well," she sighed, "that's the past for you."

Tommy might have invented the story to give a struggling business some added romance—or added value. But if it was a hype to jack up the price of the bar, why refuse to sell? And if nothing was buried beneath the weeds in that crumbling parking lot, what was everyone getting so excited about?

The woman from the title company commanded me to help her replace four more tomes on shelves even higher than before. I went away covered in the dust of dead records that had lost their meaning many years ago.

I dragged myself back to the office. A certain amount of mopping up was inevitable, and the longer I waited, the dirtier a job it would be.

This time it was Art Shade, the bailbondsman, who had my messages. He held up a fistful of pink slips, his body filling the doorway. The fat used to be muscle; Shade had been a bounty hunter for other bailbondsmen before he started his own firm. Now, with his wide polyester lapels

69

and orange-tinted glasses, he looked more like a used-carpet salesman.

"They've been coming in all morning," he said. "This whole thing stands to get outta hand, don'tcha think?"

"I didn't talk to any reporters. I mean I didn't *know* he was a reporter."

"Well, whatever, but you're gonna have to do something to stop tying up my phone lines. I can't do business if there's a hunnerd people trying to get through to you when you're not around. Guy on TV said people are swarming all over that parking lot, trying to dig it up. Looks like you really started something."

"The whole thing ought to die down in a day or so." What a ridiculous, impossibly hopeful thought. I took the messages and started upstairs.

"Hey!" he said after me. "Is there really a buncha money buried out there?"

I shook my head and kept going.

"And Cass!"

This time I stopped.

"You still vacating your office on the thirtieth?"

Three and a half weeks away. "Yeah. I'll be out of here."

"Unnerstand, I'm not asking you to leave or nothing. . . ."

"I understand. I've been planning this for a long time."

"We'll miss you, you know that."

"Sure. And Art?"

"Yeah?"

"Is anybody up there waiting for me?"

"Not so far as I know."

Thank God.

The name of Michael Sloane stood out prominently from the stack of two dozen phone messages. Time to face the situation. Pick up the phone and get it over with.

"What in fucking hell was that story?" Michael's voice blasted out over the telephone. "I ask you to look for Tommy Malakis *quietly*, and you mouth off to a reporter! What did you do, whisper to him?"

70

"It wasn't like that—"

"What's it matter? Now *everybody* knows he's alive!"

"I don't know that's true. I was just at the Hall of Records, and it looks like the whole thing could be a sham—"

"You played right into the hands of the builders, you know that, don't you? Now what are we going to do? How are we going to repair this, this, disaster? Just tell me that!"

I took a breath. "What do you care? You wanted your goddamn three-ring circus. Now you've got it. Why complain?"

"What are you saying to me now? That *we're* the bad guys? This coalition is barely alive, in case you weren't aware. We're up against a multi-fucking-million-dollar corporation here. They are out to bury this neighborhood. And we've got to have weapons!"

"Tommy Malakis is not a 'weapon.' And he's got no reason to come to you, he'll know that by now."

"Thanks to you. Look, Cass, you've blown the job as far as I can see, so we're going to send you a check for your time and just go on by ourselves. Maybe we can salvage something out of this, I don't know. But as far as I'm concerned, your involvement ends right now."

"Fine. And forget the check." I hung up on him. So much for Tommy Malakis. The possibility of helping him had vanished. There was the slightest chance that the treasure story was bona fide, but Tommy Malakis wouldn't be seeing any of the money. He was better off missing.

Three of the messages were from Sonia, spaced twenty minutes apart, and every one was marked URGENT. I picked up the phone again and prepared to tell her that the date for my departure from San Francisco was being moved up.

She interrupted before I could speak. "Cass," she said. Her voice was shaking, and she sounded on the verge of tears. "Oh, God. Have you heard?"

"Forget it, Sonia. The whole thing's a scam anyway. If Tommy Malakis knows what's good for him, he'll stay far away. Assuming he's alive, that is. Anyway, I'm getting out—"

71

"You had better come across the street, Cass. Sherman Tuttle has been murdered."

Tuttle? What the hell has that got to do with Malakis? That was my first crazy thought. My second was of the felt pens. Dazzling colors, dozens of them, all spread out like a peacock's tail. Every one had a purpose. He had a way of sweeping them off the desk with a flourish, then locking his briefcase with a snap. . . .

"Cass? They found his body . . . most of it . . . in a dumpster. He was stabbed . . . please get over here. Oh God, I'm sorry. . . ."

I couldn't stop staring out the window. The Potrero Hill smokestack was obscured by a milky haze. It shimmered and shifted; my eyes wouldn't focus. And the blinding void had a familiar voice. *I wanted to thank you for what you did*, it told me, just like one year ago. Then it smiled, if it is possible for a voice to smile.

Finally I turned away and went down the stairs. Adrian called out, waving little pink pieces of paper. Outside it was too bright to see. The alley leading out to Bryant Street was still in the sickening heaviness of the afternoon. A van was blocking the far end. The idea of talking to Sonia, of telling her I had ignored the pleas of a murdered man, was unbearable. I was his protector and I had failed to protect. People die when you care and when you believe. And they die when you don't. It didn't seem to make any difference. Whatever made me think that running away from the P.D.'s office would prevent it from happening again?

I wish that van would get out of the way, I thought, unable to comprehend that it was only blocking the alley to other cars, not people. Plenty of room to get around it. So why were there no people? The merest physical detail struck me as an impenetrable mystery. Why is no one in that car? And why is this arm reaching out from a doorway and grabbing me, pulling me in? And why can't I scream? But I knew the answer to that question. Because a fist had smashed me in the throat. I was gagging, my stomach was heaving, how could I possibly be expected to scream under such circumstances?

72

Now I was being slammed against a brick wall. Somehow I knew it was brick. My senses had recovered miraculously from the shock of learning that Sherman Tuttle had been murdered. All sensations were clear now. Only they seemed to consist entirely of pain—one singing wire of pain that stretched the length of my body. I desperately wanted to throw up, as if that would relieve everything. A kick in the stomach finally made it possible. Then the wire snapped.

Part Two

11

"I'll kill the son of a bitch!"

Joseph slammed his fist down on the Formica so hard that the entire booth rattled, causing pain to shoot up my ribs and down my arm. I sucked in air and waited for the shock to subside.

"Oh Jesus, Cass, I'm real sorry, I didn't mean to do that." Joseph grabbed the table to stop it from vibrating. It didn't help. "It's just that it really burns me to see you like this, and if I catch the motherfucker who did it I'll twist his fool head off. Just watch me!"

"I'd rather not." I took a napkin and mopped at the spilled coffee. The alarms that had been installed in my nervous system were quiet again. If I didn't move, I would be fine.

"Joseph, please," said my mother. "The language." I was sitting across from her in the booth, staring at a cold cup of coffee on a sluggish Sunday afternoon. All things considered, it seemed like a good way to spend the next twenty years.

"Sorry." Joseph stalked back to the grill, still fuming.

"Aunt Brigid's been asking why you don't come and see her," my mother continued. "It's so beautiful out there this time of year. And quiet too."

"I'll think about it." I was half listening to her and half assessing the damage to my body for the five hundredth time. Ribs: three broken. They couldn't be bandaged, so I had to take shallow breaths to avoid the slicing pain. Arm: jammed finger and sprained wrist wrapped in splint and Ace bandage. Huge, ugly purple and yellow bruises. Not black and blue, as they usually describe it. Head: the kind of marks you get from rubbing your face against a brick wall; a migraine that ranged between throbbing and unbearable. Eye: swollen. That was the softball injury. Funny how I used to think it hurt.

". . . you wouldn't have to worry at all, we can take care of the restaurant. She gets so lonely up there, and seeing you would just brighten her day—"

"Mother, you've been trying to get me out of town for months and Aunt Brigid has nothing to do with it. Why don't you just say it? You're worried about me, I look like hell, and I need to recuperate in some pastoral sanatorium."

"That's your decision. I would never tell you what to do, I'm not that kind of mother—"

"Every mother is that kind of mother. Look, I know what the doctor said. I need a month on my back. If I came down with the vapors, he'd say I needed a month on my back."

"There's no need to be flippant. Two weeks ago you were ready to pack your bags. Now you just sit there . . . wait a minute, I think I know. . . ."

"Do tell. I'm dying to know myself."

"You've met someone. Someone in the city."

"Oh come on, Mother—"

"And you're keeping it a secret again. Another boyfriend who's allergic to garlic?"

"You know damned well I haven't 'met someone' for more than a year. Now will you please leave me alone? You're not helping, so just keep it to yourself, all right?"

Even as I said the words I wanted to take them back. Too late. My mother had donned her cloak of martyrdom, the look of a woman bearing the sins of the world. Our Lady of Columbus Avenue. By keeping quiet, she could make me feel even guiltier. And because she was doing it on purpose, I refused to give her the satisfaction of an apology. Of course that made me feel even worse.

"While you're gone, we can have the house painted and the rewiring done," she said, passing over my rudeness. "Maybe Sara would be willing to put you up a little early. . . ."

I wasn't listening anymore. For some reason it hurt to listen, so I fixed on the far wall of the Nick of America and studied the row of softball trophies and game balls that shared a shelf with jug wine and cans of olive oil. The grimy interior was warm and friendly. Why not live right here? I could hide out in the storeroom. No need to send for food. My eyes shifted from the walls back to my mother, then to the open purse beside me in the booth, and the gun inside it. Elroy's gift. *You be needing it, I'm sure.* The nostalgia passed. There was nothing I wanted more than to follow my mother's poorly veiled advice.

"I have to stay in town for a while," I told her, "and that's all there is to it."

"Well, what should I tell Aunt Brigid?" my mother was saying when I noticed Eddie squinting through the window. Joseph saw him at the same instant and charged into the street, grabbing my ex-husband by the ornamental rings of his prestressed leather jacket. "Joseph, stop!" I yelled, but he couldn't hear me through the glass. His face was inches from Eddie's, and they were deep in conversation. Then he began shaking Eddie like a can of paint. Groaning in the agony of movement, I dragged myself out of the booth, my mother following.

"Joseph, please!" I managed to gasp. "Leave him alone. I asked him to come."

Joseph and my mother exchanged a look of panic, but the big man stopped manhandling Eddie. "Come on inside," I said to the cringing figure. Trying his best to regain some self-respect, Eddie smoothed his pomp and followed me back to the booth, Joseph glaring from the doorway. My protector was so keyed up about murdering the man who had assaulted me that he seemed perfectly happy to kill Eddie as a substitute.

"My God, Cass, he needs to be put in a cage or something, you know?" Eddie took my mother's place in the booth as I reassembled my broken body across from him. "Fucking gorilla. Hey, you think I could get some hot coffee here?"

Joseph and my mother were doing a poor job of concealing themselves behind the hanging saucepans. "No, I don't think you could," I said. At least not in a cup.

"Shit. Listen, you still got that roll of film?"

"It hasn't gone anywhere."

"Well, have it developed for me, okay? If I'm seen carrying it around, those two thugs'll be on me in a second. I'm thinking of doing like a documentary or something on insurance scams. Like a '60 Minutes' kinda thing, hidden cameras, busting into their offices. I'm gonna nail their asses, and you can help me do it."

"First things first. You owe me a favor."

"Huh? I helped you out already."

"And screwed it up. Now I'm giving you a chance to make up for your little mistake with the reporter."

"Hey, come on now, I told you about that—"

"Shut up and listen. It's real simple. I need a photograph of a man."

"So send him to me."

"I don't think he'll pose. For one thing, you can't let him know you're taking his picture. He might not appreciate it."

"If you're getting me into trouble here—"

"Not if you stay out of it. A shot from a distance with a long lens will do just fine. He hangs around South of Market. I last saw him outside the detox center on Folsom a week ago. He's six three or four, two hundred twenty pounds, very pale skin, crew cut, white hair. Forty, maybe forty-five. Kind of an intense look. Like I said, don't get too close. Just bring me a picture."

"You gonna tell me who he is, or do I find out when he tries to bash my skull in? Come to think of it, is this the guy you think—"

"I'm sure you can do it, Eddie." He lived in an artist's loft not far from where I had seen the strange man following Harry Cremmins and me. "Nose around quietly. You'll come up with something."

I was starting to sound like Michael Sloane, but it was the only lead. While I hadn't gotten a look at the person who attacked me, that white-haired zombie could have managed it without too much trouble. Only he wasn't in any of the mug books, and the cops had shown little interest in my description.

"I'd be better off poking through garbage cans." Eddie squeezed out of the booth, shoving the table against my ribs. The eyes of Joseph and my mother followed him out of the restaurant. Let them think what they wanted. I pushed back the table with my good arm and wished the pain away. The gun had slipped from my purse when I rose to save Eddie's life. I put it back. I'm not so bad off, I kept telling myself. Sherman Tuttle was stabbed twenty times, both hands cut off. One of them was still missing. The other was stuffed down his throat. Coroner couldn't be sure whether he bled to death or choked to death. A mental note: Call Sara Ludlow in Santa Rosa, tell her I'll be delayed in the city for a while. Due to unfinished business.

The next morning I dropped off Eddie's roll of film at a one-hour photo lab on my way to Sherman Tuttle's former residence. It had only been four days since the murder—my immobility made it feel like weeks—but the police had already left it alone. After all, it was nothing but the murder of a crazy man.

Tuttle's hotel room was in the heart of South of Market's sleaze, on Sixth below Market. A block away was Wino Park, where Malakis—or someone—had been incinerated. A grand experiment by civic leaders, the park had been closed two years ago after turning into the neighborhood's outdoor supermarket for mind-altering substances.

A big bald man wielding a broomstick was blocking the hotel's doorway. He was facing off against a derelict.

"Piss in this doorway and I'll take your head off!" the man with the broomstick was saying.

"Oh yeah? Maybe I *wanna* piss in it," the bum whined. "What choo think of that?"

"I'll tell you exactly what I think! If this keeps up, we'll *both* have to go to the hospital. You for an autopsy, and me to have my *boot* removed from your *ass!*"

"Oh yeah?" said the bum, holding his position unsteadily while considering a snappy rejoinder. "Well . . . what if I do it *anyway*?"

I pushed past them and climbed the stairs to the third floor. The lock had been broken, and the door opened easily. Before me were the remnants of Sherman Tuttle's life—smashed to bits.

The police had said only that the room was "disturbed" shortly after the estimated time of Tuttle's death. They've got to be kidding, I thought, surveying the shredded heaps of cloth and paper that covered the floor. Here were his laboriously constructed charts, destroyed. Felt pens were everywhere, and those awful clothes—checks, plaids, paisleys. As if they had torn to pieces the man himself. But then of course they had.

I sifted through the meaningless debris. Most of the scraps had numbers scribbled on them, in an array of colors. And there were the implements of everyday life: the hot plate, the plastic bowls and silverware, the girlie magazines, the tiny black-and-white television with a broken antenna, probably fished out of a dumpster. In this room Tuttle had nurtured his paranoia, let it run wild, until it killed him. Thanks to me.

The wreckage spoke of rage—the rage of someone looking for a particular object or piece of information. Evidence that could be used against him. To stab a helpless, mentally impaired man so many times . . . and to cut off his hands . . .

The handcuffs. Tuttle must have had the briefcase locked to his wrist. The murderer sliced off his hand to get it. Then he cut off the other hand to make it look like senseless brutality. But if he then broke into this room and tore it to pieces . . . the killer hadn't found everything he was looking for. Tuttle had hidden his "evidence" elsewhere. I felt in my pocket for the dirty envelope he had given me the last time I saw him. There was a key inside and I tried it in the door.

It didn't fit.

I wasn't surprised. It had an orange plastic handle and the number 714 engraved in it. More like the key to a safe-deposit box, or a public locker.

When I got home there was a message on my machine from Michael Sloane. He wanted to see me.

12

I didn't call Michael back. I was off the Malakis case, and there was no reason to speak to him. As far as I was concerned, only two items of business had to be tackled before I could quit San Francisco once and for all: clear up Eddie's "insurance" troubles, and find the murderer of Sherman Tuttle. I didn't need the additional complication of a case on which I had already screwed up. By firing me, Michael had done me a favor.

Returning from Tuttle's room empty-handed left my evening open. I had nothing but a locker key without a lock. Tomorrow I would search the city.

I was finding it difficult to concentrate my energies on any one thing these days. The postponed departure from San Francisco had left me in limbo. I wasn't going to the "office" anymore. In the last few days my time had been divided between the Nick of America and home, where I could kill hours at a time by tinkering with the jukeboxes in my garage. There were eleven of them, ranging from a '55 Seeburg to a Wurlitzer replica from the early seventies. They were left over from another one of Eddie's scams, and when it went bust shortly before our marriage broke up, I was the one who learned to fix them. In recent months the jukeboxes had become necessary therapy. Now, even though my movements were severely curtailed, I managed to tinker around. Pain or no pain, it was the only activity that I could sustain for more than fifteen minutes without giving up in a fit of restlessness. The intricate mechanics of the work dulled my mind, stopped it from dwelling on the agonies of the last year.

Which is why I didn't notice Michael Sloane standing in the garage until he punched up a lousy Tony Bennett song. Startled, I pulled on the injured ribs again, and swore at the pain.

"Hell of a greeting," he said.

"Wasn't meant for you. Although it should have been."

"I won't say you're wrong. Anyway, I saw the garage door open, so I came in. Sorry if I scared you."

I gave my attention back to the jukebox. The pump was busted, so the bubbles wouldn't flow. And the fluorescent tubes would have to be replaced with real tinted ones. This one had white tubes wrapped in colored paper. Strictly amateur restoration work.

"Actually, I'm sorry for a lot more than that," Michael said as Tony Bennett warbled "I Left My Heart in San Francisco." I've always hated that song. "I'll tell you right now, I was a real asshole."

"Were you?"

I had never seen Michael in such a contrite mood. His hands were shoved in the back pockets of his jeans, and he kept looking at the ground. "That Cremmins guy disappeared the other day," he said. "Walked out of The Wayside and I haven't seen him since."

I tried to pretend that my attention was captured by the guts of the jukebox. In reality, I couldn't even align the screwdriver with the head slot. I was fighting to keep myself under control again.

Michael squatted beside me. "Come on, Cass. We've known each other a long time. Don't let a little thing like this get in the way of a friendship."

The screwdriver flew out of my hand. It missed Michael's head by inches. He flinched, but otherwise froze to the spot. I guess I had thrown it.

85

"'Asshole' isn't the word for you," I murmured.

I'm snapping at last, I thought. The slightest thing will set me off and I'm not sure I can stop it from happening. I've got to get out of this city.

"Get lost," I said.

Michael didn't move. "You see what's happening, don't you? First that note from Malakis, then Tuttle gets murdered—that's no coincidence, Cass."

"I don't see the connection."

"That's 'cause you're not looking. We're trying to stop this development and somebody would like to stop *us*."

Michael would interpret an earthquake as God's personal vendetta against him. "Your evil developers again?"

"If somebody wants to discredit what we do at The Wayside, what better way than to stir up all this shit?"

"Would you believe I don't care?"

"Bullshit. You couldn't walk away now even if you wanted to. Face it, Cass. We're a couple of guilty Catholics."

"Speak for yourself."

"What about Sherman Tuttle?"

"What about him?"

"Guess you don't care about him either."

"Fuck you." I wiped my hands and headed for the kitchen.

"All right, that was a low blow. But how do you think I feel? It was my place he was hanging around. And I'm the one sent him to you. Anyway, I know you're already on the case, so why can't we work together?"

"Who told you that?"

"You paid Art Shade for another month, didn't you?"

Of course he would know a thing like that. Tony Bennett finally shut up, then started again, singing about the goddamn loveliness of Paris. This was the jukebox with the broken changer, causing it to play the same record over and over. An appropriate malfunction. Solving the Tuttle "case" seemed like an endless task. But I had to do it for myself, not for Michael Sloane.

"Let me hire you. We both need an answer. At the very least let me cover your expenses. Okay?"

I pulled the plug on Tony and went into the house.

*　　*　　*

The crowd outside the bus station was more than the usual bums, pimps, hawkers, and students with backpacks. Tourists who had strayed from Market Street were being held back by strips of yellow tape that said POLICE LINE: DO NOT CROSS. Rubberneckers. I shouldered my way through the crowd and presented my public defender's I.D. to the cop guarding the entrance.

"So?" he said, barely looking at the card.

"I'm here on official business. Please let me through."

"Guy don't need a lawyer." He shrugged and stepped aside.

Another crowd was gathered at the back of the station. There were reporters, paramedics, cops, bus drivers. Through the shifting bodies I could see an aluminum stretcher being unfolded. An ambulance waited, lights flashing through the dank and chilly boarding area.

Somebody asked the people to make way. The paramedics guided the gurney out of the throng, and it rattled past. The body was covered by a darkly stained sheet. The entourage followed.

I asked a reporter what happened.

"Wino sleeping under a bus," he said, backing away. "Driver started it up this morning without knowing."

The reporter disappeared and the gawkers returned to their waiting lanes, still murmuring about the accident. They stood with their suitcases under weather-beaten signs that announced destinations like Eureka, Yountville, Fresno, and Santa Rosa.

In the alley stood a bus with a reddish-black trail behind it, like a oil stain. He must have been dragged thirty feet at least. What a stupid place to sleep.

The station lockers ran the length of the back wall. I took out the key with the orange plastic handle and checked the number again: 714. I looked around to make certain that no one was watching. Tuttle's paranoia was contagious.

The locker was toward the end, in the lower left-hand corner about six inches off the ground. Damn you, Sherman, I thought, you did this on purpose. I squatted painfully and, after some effort, managed to unlock it.

It was filled with junk: candy wrappers, a half-eaten doughnut crawling with ants, more felt pens, a torn tennis shoe, and the usual pile of papers covered with hieroglyphics. Discarded efforts. This secret storage place appeared to be more of a waste can, containing none of the bursts of multicolored minutiae that were the real products of Tuttle's madness.

I stuck my hand in further, feeling soft and sticky shapes. Here was more food—I couldn't tell what kind—and some old socks. Then something that looked like a penlight. On closer examination I recognized it as one of those "Man from U.N.C.L.E." spy pens that they used to advertise in the comic books. See through walls, see around corners. Always wanted one when I was a kid. I put it in my pocket.

After a couple more shuffles the corner of an envelope appeared. I pulled it from the gunk and shook off the ants. Tore off a corner and out dropped another key.

It too had a number—506—but the handle was black plastic, and the key was slightly larger than the orange one. Obviously it went to another bank of lockers.

My spirits sank at the prospect of one key leading to another, an endless series of doors behind doors. I closed the locker and pocketed both keys. How many lockers were there in San Francisco? Or, for that matter, how far afield had Tuttle ranged? The Bay Area? The entire state? I could imagine his ravings scribbled down and distributed among a thousand dirty hiding places across the nation.

There has to be a better way than driving all over the Bay Area, I thought as I walked back through the station. The answer was sitting in the ticket lobby, watching television.

There were two rows of TV sets bolted to the plastic seats like an extra appendage. For twenty-five cents you could kill fifteen minutes watching fuzzy black-and-white shows.

Bored passengers weren't the only ones who watched. On most weekdays you could find an aging bag lady glued to the last seat in the first row—"the one with the best reception," she always claimed. Everybody called her Hollywood Alice;

she watched six game shows a day, celebrating with the winners and commiserating with the losers. The rest of her waking hours were spent panhandling for money to feed the TV.

Like Tuttle, Alice was a pack rat, with caches of "valuables" all over town. I found her in her usual place, surrounded by shopping bags. The TV was bursting with laughter and applause.

"Oh, hello, miss," she said. "This is quite a day, isn't it?"

"Not for that man," I said, gesturing in the direction of the boarding area.

"Oh, no, it's wonderful. The Roseburgs have won sixty-five thousand dollars in three days, and a mobile home too! But then the Dohertys aren't doing so well. They didn't know who was vice president under Harry Truman. Do you?"

"Alice." I held out the key with the black handle. "Do you know where these lockers are?"

She looked at the key for half a second and turned her attention back to the TV. "Cruise ship terminal. Pier 35."

If she said so. "Thank you."

"But wait. I have something to show you." She started picking through a bag at her feet, casting aside pieces of yarn, coat hangers, and newspapers.

"Just one sec. . . . Here it is." She pulled out a newspaper page and folded it back. "Listen to this, hon. There's a new book out about Princess Grace and the author says . . . let me just find it . . . he says, 'She sacrificed her career and suffered for it, but it was her decision. Sometimes she was very lonely, and sometimes she had fantasies of being poor, of being a bag lady.'"

"Isn't that something."

"Yes, isn't it?" Alice folded the paper neatly and slipped it back in the bag with a smile. "Just think—Princess Grace would dream of being *me!*"

"Thanks for the tip." I handed her a dollar.

"Anytime."

From the outside, the cruise terminal was just another waterfront warehouse. It sat on one of the finger piers along the

89

northeastern waterfront that used to constitute the center of the Bay Area's shipping activity. Over the years they had either burned down or been converted into tourist attractions, and most of San Francisco's commercial shipping had long since migrated across the Bay to Oakland.

Inside, the terminal was a far cry from the bus station. The port had coughed up the money to install carpets and banners and lounges for the cruise set, who traveled to Alaska in the summer and the Caribbean in the winter. The bus riders had only Yountville.

The lockers were smartly painted and protected from the elements. I wondered how people like Sherman Tuttle and Hollywood Alice were received in this environment of romantic globetrotters. Somehow they managed to mingle, for the second key fit locker 506, and another pile of rubbish spilled out.

A couple of used felt pens. An unmatched driving glove with holes cut at the knuckles. An unused but expired roll of Polaroid film. Some matchbook covers. And something that looked familiar: an eight-track tape with Chinese writing on it.

Funny, I thought, it's just like the tapes in my office, left by the previous tenant. Only this one isn't in its cardboard box. Tuttle, when he was alone in my office, could easily have taken the tape and left the box behind.

Maybe it was a trade.

I rushed to the office, afraid that someone had gotten smart and searched the place. But nothing unusual greeted me when I finally made it up the stairs, past the familiar odors, and unlocked the door. There was the same barren, characterless room. The flowers in the bottle of Night Train were desiccated sticks, their shriveled petals lying on the desk. It was the first time I had set foot in the office since being attacked, and it wasn't a welcome sight.

I plowed through the pile of eight-track tapes. They all pictured what I assumed to be Chinese pop stars, sporting big smiles and surrounded by wild lettering. A few tapes into the pile I started to recognize three or four recurring artists. They must be the biggies, I thought.

Finally, at the bottom of the stack, I found it: a tape box that contained a small spiral notebook, the kind you can buy at any stationery store. Filled with colorful numbers and letters, it contained the secrets of Sherman Tuttle—in code.

13

I couldn't understand any of it. The letters were arranged in blocks of five, and colored, apparently, at random. An occasional period took up a full space in the cipher blocks. Four or five numbers were inscribed at the top of each page. I knew that you could solve ciphers by calculating the frequency of various letters in the message, but Tuttle's use of different colors added an enormous complication. I sat at the desk and took a crack at it anyway.

Page 1 began with the numbers 39.3.1. Following that were colored letters: an orange I, a purple A, a green E, and so on. There were fourteen blocks in all—including the numbers at the beginning—the last block consisting of only three letters.

He was using seven colors, and their sequence had to be crucial. I suddenly wished that I had his damned felt pens.

I copied the code from the first page onto another sheet of paper. Because I had nothing but a pen with blue ink, I designated the color of each letter by an initial beneath it: R for red, Y for yellow, B for blue, O for orange, P for purple, G for green, and K for black. It looked like this:

39.3.1 IAEED   .CMNO SSSLS ERLRD MNWYO MASN.
        OPGPG   KRPG   GRYGP YYRYG OPOPP GKBK

EED.C MNOSS SLSA. TOKIO   WNORM EAE.L WCN
YPG K RPGGR YGGP   OOKKY   OOYOG YPR R BKG

It was hopeless. Without the key I couldn't even begin to decipher it. And who was to say that it made sense anyway? Tuttle's grasp of logic was tenuous at best.

A call from Eddie, believe it or not, provided a merciful respite.

"Cass? I got those pictures you wanted. At least I think it's the guy. I'm gonna develop them tonight. Meet me at Wilma's, tomorrow at lunchtime. Bring the accident pictures. And don't tell anyone you're coming, for Chrissake."

Sonia and I settled into a table at Wilma's and waited for Eddie. I would need Sonia's help for the next phase.

I ordered my usual: grilled cheese on rye, fruit salad, french fries, and iced tea. Sonia got a patty melt with extra grease. For a moment I was back at the P.D.'s office, grabbing lunch across the street from the Hall while court was in recess. Wilma's hadn't changed: the same murky aquarium, sparkle ceiling, and upright piano, which Early Times occasionally played for tips. But the differences were too obvious to sustain the illusion. There was Sonia, dressed for trial in a conservative blue patterned dress with black suede jacket, string of pearls, and heels. And me, in blue jeans, running shoes, and a wrinkled cotton blouse, the easiest thing to put on in the morning, given my injuries. I felt left out of things.

At first I thought the man in sunglasses walking through the door was a bum in search of charity. Then I recognized Eddie, his face puffed and bruised, and a surgical bandage plastered above one eye. He came over and set down a smashed Nikon.

"Hi, girls," he said. "Mind if I sit?"

"What have they done to your pretty face?" asked Sonia.

"My God," I said. Somehow, I knew how he felt. "When did this happen?"

"Last night, not long after I called you. Of course it was those two pieces of shit who want my pictures. They said if I didn't hand 'em over they'd break my legs. Like they were outta some movie or something."

"Well, you look terrible," I said.

"Same to you. You know how long it's gonna take me to heal up? And I got a business to run!"

"If you ask me, it's a business you should consider retiring from."

"Eah, it's no big deal. I said I didn't have the pictures, they said I was lying, we went back and forth on that for a while. Then they knocked me around, figured I was telling the truth, and split. Real tough guys."

"Then you won't mind taking these off my hands." I slid over the envelope with the prints from Eddie's much-desired role of film. It didn't show a lot: a couple of smashed bumpers and a street full of headlight glass. Eddie was never that good a photographer.

He didn't touch the envelope right away. "I don't know, Cass, maybe you should—"

"Take them. I've had my quota of beatings for the month."

He complied with a mournful look.

"What about *my* pictures?" I asked. "Did anything survive your little run-in last night?"

"Oh, they redecorated my darkroom, but I already had these developed. Hey, let me get a beer here or something, I'm dying of thirst."

"That probably wouldn't be a good idea," said Sonia. "Earl was asking about you a couple of days ago. Said you'd run up quite a tab."

Eddie looked over his shoulder. "Earl's just a little impatient. Anyway, here they are." He withdrew a sheaf of black-and-white photos from a manila envelope and spread them on the table. "I shot a few possibilities."

"Wow," said Sonia. "Portraits of life, South of the Slot. Very attractive."

There were a variety of men who more or less answered the description I had given Eddie. They were taken outside shelters, in the parks, on the street. Most were poorly

94

framed, as if snapped in haste. This man was too short, another too fat, still another had hair that was too long. All were bums, and the sinister man I had seen didn't fit that label. More like a psycho.

Here was a familiar face. It was Harry Cremmins, leaning against a rusting city bus. "Where did you take this one?"

"Oh yeah, that's this old bus that the city parked under the freeway near the creek. So bums can have a place to sleep."

"I heard about that," Sonia said. "Supposed to be temporary while they looked around for more beds. Classy accommodations, aren't they?"

I didn't understand. "But why did you take a picture of Harry Cremmins? He doesn't look anything like the man I described."

"That his name? I don't know, but it's not a picture of *him*. Check out the guy behind, that's who I was shooting."

I looked more closely. Because of poor light and a long lens, it was difficult to make out anyone in the background. Difficult, but not impossible. Standing some distance away was the man I wanted.

"What was Cremmins doing there?" I asked Eddie. "Do you know?"

"Living, I guess. You think I walked up and asked him?"

I passed the picture to Sonia. My hand was shaking. "See this guy with the white hair standing way off to the side? You know him?"

Sonia angled the picture to cut the glare. "My God, girl, what are you messing around with *him* for?"

"Who is he?"

"Not *my* client, thank goodness. I think Larry Sylvester has represented him a couple of times? He's a real nut. Did you know that? You mean this is the man who attacked you?"

"He's the only possibility I know of."

"Well, he is *wacko*. What's his name now? O'Grady? O'Flaherty? Geraghty. Gerald Geraghty, that's it. Larry had him on a couple of assault cases—mostly for beating up on other bums for no particular reason. You better stay away from him."

The police report said Gerald Geraghty was a friend of Reuben Murtaugh, casualty of the Leeward Inn fire. I felt a sudden chill. Some people blamed Tommy Malakis for that fire. A short time later he, or somebody, was burned to death in Wino Park. Maybe it was an insane man's idea of justice. And the man who might have been Malakis's tormentor was now following Harry Cremmins.

Eddie stared at the picture. "You mean this guy is some crazy-ass killer, and you had me tailing him? Thanks one helluva lot!"

"Cass, what are you going to do?" asked Sonia. "Shouldn't you give this picture to the police?"

"They don't give a damn. Besides, there's no proof. He's just another bum as far as they're concerned."

"But if this is the guy who beat up—"

"Maybe, maybe not."

"What do you mean?"

"I've got to find Harry Cremmins." Like it or not, I was back on the Malakis case.

14

According to the file that Sonia pulled from the public defender's office, Gerald Geraghty was a borderline psychotic who had been in and out of hospitals for twenty years. He was a member of that fringe group that even the regular bums stayed away from, one of the really dangerous types who had slipped through a crack in the underbudgeted system. It was a vicious circle: crazy people were living on the street, and living on the street made you crazy.

You could see them every day, staggering along the street or huddled in the corner of a park. Their insanity took many forms—here a strung-out twenty-year-old muttering under his breath, there an old lady tearing up the brick sidewalks on Market Street. Sometimes they would slip out of control, or their meds would wear off, and they would go screaming down the block. Sherman Tuttle was one of them.

The Municipal bus that had been set aside as shelter for the bums stood mired in mud under the freeway, beside a dirty creek. Green and beige were barely visible through the corrosion and rust. Muni buses hadn't been those colors for at least fifteen years.

A derelict squatted before a rubbish fire. An old man in an army jacket with a bandage wrapped around his head was passed out in the bus's doorway, just like in Eddie's photo.

The place was a hobo jungle in the middle of the city, the Depression relived. I stepped over the comatose man and climbed aboard the bus.

Seats were slashed, the rubber floor was encrusted with dirt, and ripped cardboard ads dangled over the windows. The smell was unbearable.

On the rear seat was a lump covered by newspapers. I went toward it.

I heard the traffic overhead and the rhythmic clanking of a sailboat's rigging from somewhere down the creek. The lump lay motionless.

A hand protruded from the newspapers. I touched the yellowed paper. Took a single sheet between two fingers and pulled, and the whole pile sloughed off, exposing the face of Harry Cremmins.

It was a ghastly face, pasty and bloated. I stood over the body for what seemed like a long time. Then Cremmins emitted a sonorous, rumbling belch.

Kicking the rest of the papers away, I shook his shoulder. He came alive with an assortment of intestinal noises, and it was a full minute before he could assemble fragments of reality and recognize me standing before him.

"Oh my God," he mumbled. "How in hell . . . you find me." He buried his face in a rag. "Why can't all people leave me alone."

He was numbingly drunk. "Why did you run away from The Wayside?" I demanded. "Who are you hiding from?"

Cremmins propped himself and rubbed his face with a blackened hand. He wiped the hand on his pants. "I gotta beef with your paper," he said hazily. "Don't like to get dirty sleeping in it. They tell me it's a question a how long the ink's gotta dry. You want a better paper it's a printer's problem. Cheap. . . . Cheapskates."

I shoved aside a heap of rags and settled into the seat in front of him. "Is Tommy Malakis alive?"

"Ukiah can get out a paper that don't make your hands dirty." He broke into a coughing jag. "I'm just looking for some peace and quiet."

"You'll never find it if you don't answer my questions."

"You can't threaten me," Cremmins growled. "Get outta my way." His feeble effort to rise got him halfway there before I pushed him back down.

He grunted as he sank into the trash. "Leave me alone!"

"Tell me more about Malakis."

"I told you, we was friends—"

"Notice anybody following you lately, Harry?"

The question threw him into abject silence.

"Seen Tommy lately?"

"He's dead, goddamn it."

"When did you stop working at the bar?"

"What bar. Already told you that."

What did he have against Malakis? Chances were that Cremmins was a lush even back then. I gave it a shot. "He fired you, didn't he?"

"Huh."

"For drinking. Who was trying to buy the place?"

Cremmins stared at me, breathing hard.

"Somebody is out to kill you, Harry. Who tried to buy the bar from Malakis?"

"Don't know."

"You burned it down, didn't you?"

"No!" He was really scared. "Guy I knew came in, made an offer. Kept on asking. Tommy didn't know him. I did. He owned a hotel round here, name was Virgil . . . Whaley. Told me keep my damn mouth shut."

"Which hotel?"

"The D-D-Doyle. But I ain't seen him for years. Disappeared right after the bar burned down. That's when I got the hell outta town. Knew if I stayed . . . might disappear too. You . . . know what I mean."

"This Virgil Whaley warned you to keep quiet?"

Cremmins was starting to sweat. "Saw him coupla times in the bar. Knew him 'cause I lived in his fucking pigsty for a while. He never told Tommy his real name."

"Why didn't you?"

"Why should I!" he burst out. "Fucker fired me, all right, but . . . I *wasn't* drunk on the job . . . damn lie. Just a few drinks, here and there. Just to keep going. I mean a coupla lousy shots a . . . That was the last job I ever had, you know that? Never worked again, couldn't get nobody to . . ."

His eyes filled with tears of self-pity. "And Whaley," I prompted.

"And Whaley, he comes up to me after trying to buy the place and says, 'You keep quiet about this, Harry.' Fine with me, what do I give a shit. Then poof, place goes up in smoke. Then Whaley was gone too. Didn't wanna be next, you know what I mean. So I left town."

"*After* the bar burned down."

"Okay, after . . . I get confused sometimes!"

"But now all of a sudden you decided to come back? Just like that?"

"Nooo. I just thought, it's been so long, it'd be safe to come back and look for that money, I thought no one would still remember, but I was fucking wrong, now somebody's after *me*, some crazy . . ."

Cremmins collapsed into alcoholic sobs. I left him in the back of the bus, huddled on the floor, inexplicably clinging to what remained of his miserable life.

The boy behind the registration desk of the Doyle Hotel was about ten years old and looked Indian. The smell of cigarettes was heavy in the air. He was reading a math book, and he ignored me the first two times I addressed him. On the third try he looked up. "What did you say?" he snapped.

"I said, 'Excuse me, I need some help.'"

He shrugged and went back to the book. The hotel lobby was no better or worse than any other in the neighborhood: cracked vinyl couch repaired with duct tape, broken TV set in one corner, broken cigarette machine in another, and registration counter shoved under the stairs with a wall of empty pigeonholes behind it. On the wall hung a calendar from a Mexican restaurant, with a busty woman in a torn skirt waving the Mexican flag.

I had been in this place and others like it many times before, interviewing witnesses or families of the accused who lived ten to a room and shared a bathroom with four other families. South of Market's residence hotels were home to a class of citizens one step above the street people—those with a meager welfare or disability check to pay for a room each month, who wouldn't make any trouble about the lack of heat in the winter, fans in the summer, and hot water all the time. Some of the hotels were paid by the city to take the spillover from the mental hospitals and shelters.

"Is your father around? The owner, I mean."

The kid shook his head without looking up. The rudeness was more than childish behavior. He was probably coached by the owner to ignore anybody who came around asking questions.

"He's not here, or he isn't the owner?"

"He's my uncle."

What was the point? The place had probably changed hands a dozen times since Virgil Whaley disappeared. "Investors" buy these fleabags for tax purposes, then dump them every time the city gears up one of its regular but futile urban reform campaigns. I had another idea.

"Who's lived here the longest?"

"Huh?"

"I mean which one of your guests has been here the longest time. That's not hard to figure out, is it?"

"You a cop or from welfare?"

"I'm the exterminator. Now give me a room number or I'll get the city inspectors down here to look at your boiler, your wiring, your plumbing, your rats, and whether you've been ripping off your guests' social security checks again."

The kid shrugged again and leafed through a stack of file cards. "There's a real old guy up in 412 who's been here awhile. Don't know how long."

As I climbed the stairs, the boy replaced the math book with a comic book and took a drag on a cigarette that was concealed beneath the registration desk.

The man who opened the door to Room 412 was at least sixty-five, with a couple days' growth of white beard, a thermal undershirt, and a belly bulging over pants held up by threadbare suspenders. From the room came tinny classical music. Next door, somebody was screaming.

"Yes?" He looked at me suspiciously.

I told him my name, said I wanted to ask him some questions about the hotel.

He grunted and motioned me inside. "Armstrong. *Captain* Armstrong. They're not getting my mail to me. Is that what you're here for? A million times I've complained, but they're laughing in my face. I'm expecting royalty checks. I'm a writer."

I nodded. The room was smaller than my office, with one grimy window and cut-up bedsheets for curtains. The walls were peeling to plaster and slats. A couple of black-and-white photos of battleships hung in dime-store frames. On the bedstand were a water glass, a box of tissues, and an old clock radio, source of the music. The screams were more muffled from inside the room.

"Comforts of home," he said. "Sorry about the mess. I've been working. Take a seat, please." He pointed to a folding chair with papers on it. "Just toss that stuff on the floor. You going to see to my checks?"

"Well, actually I'm here about the hotel—when it was built, who used to own it."

"How far back?"

"How long have you been here?"

"Twenty years, on and off. Since I retired from the service." He withdrew a heating coil from a mug that rested on a steamer trunk. "Tea?"

"No, thank you."

"It's Russian."

Difficult to imagine this sagging man in the service even twenty years ago, but it hardly mattered. Twenty years was long enough for my purpose.

Next door the hair-raising screams continued, punctuated by someone throwing himself against the wall. "Some wacko who got kicked out of a hospital," Captain Armstrong explained. "Goes on all night sometimes. Cops won't do a damn thing."

He settled himself on the creaky bed and tugged on a

102

beet-red earlobe. "Twenty years, that's right. I'm the only one left. Everywhere else you look, it's the goddamn Chinese, the goddamn Vietnamese. Stealing my goddamn checks."

"Then you knew Virgil Whaley?"

"Huh? . . . Sure I did. Bastard used to own this rat trap. Hell of a better place back then, of course. I'm thinking of moving."

"What happened to him?"

"There's a story there. Ran out on his wife. One day he upped and left, never came back."

"What do you mean, 'ran out'?"

"Well, I suppose just what it sounds like. Found himself a little dolly somewhere and took the chance to get away. That's what I figured. He was a mean S.O.B."

"What about the hotel?"

"Like I said, he left it to his wife. Emma. Nice gal, but no business sense at all. She was lucky to sell it. Who'd want to *buy* a place like this, I don't know. It's nowhere to live now."

His chin sank into his chest. He was lost in thought, or maybe just listening to the music, lush strings droning on. The screaming had stopped.

"Do you know who bought it?" I asked.

Captain Armstrong remembered that I was in the room. "Uh . . . one of those companies. Some real estate bastards. Anyway, who knows? All I see is Chinese, Vietnamese. That wasn't my war." He laughed. "Now it is."

Waddling over to a cardboard box, he pulled out a hardcover book.

"This is my war," he said. *Midnight to Murmansk*, it was called. The dust jacket pictured a crudely drawn ship bouncing on rough seas. It looked like a toy boat in a bathtub. MEMORIES OF THE MURMANSK RUN. BY CAPTAIN WILLIAM T. ARMSTRONG. On the back was a blurry photo of a much younger man, clutching a pipe and squinting into the camera with a cocky grin.

"Oh, sure, I call it a novel, but it's all true," he said. "I was there. The *Nathan Hale*, an old Liberty ship. We barely survived the night. The Liberties, they were beauties. Built like they make cars in Japan now, one right after the other, off the goddamn assembly line. People don't realize, but we showed the Japs how. Built to be sunk. Blast her out of the water and another one rises up to take her place. But we survived. That's what the book's about."

From the cheap quality of the book and the obscure publisher on the title page, I could tell it was the work of a "vanity press": Captain Armstrong had paid to have it published. I glanced at the five large cardboard boxes in the corner. Hundreds of copies, maybe thousands of dollars. It must have taken all the money he had.

"Sure, it was a best-seller," he said, as if reading my mind. "Into its second printing. People like the blood and guts of reality. They know when you're lying about it. There's no replacement for being there."

I put down the book. "Captain Armstrong, what happened to Emma Whaley?"

It took him a moment to change gears. "Why, she took the money and bought a house, I guess. Got out of the hotel racket. Somewhere out of San Francisco, down the peninsula, maybe San Mateo or someplace like that. Not a bad deal. Her husband was no good anyway."

I thanked him, said I had to be going. The man next door let out another scream, then was silent.

"Hold on." He started burrowing through some papers, extracting a pen from the mess. In a shaky scrawl he inscribed the flyleaf of *Midnight to Murmansk* and held out the book to me. "With my compliments. Read it, you'll learn something."

"Thank you." I accepted the free copy. Captain Armstrong was caught up in his pile of papers again. Maybe the makings of another book someday, if he could afford it.

Leaving the Doyle Hotel I passed a line of people waiting for a food giveaway. Today it was cheese—huge blocks of it, as big as bricks.

"You, you, you, you could get some *blue* cheese."

"Don't know, don't know. If that's the kind with the *mold* in it, don't think I can digest it."

The two bums coming out of the assistance office were the same pair who had sampled the doughnuts in the church vestibule. Each was lugging a hunk of the free cheese covered in food wrap.

"Well, what you want, some kinda *imported* cheese? This cheese is made in *America,* that's why it's called American. This America's cheese!"

"Sure, I know, but that don't make it right! This cheese has got *dye* in it. How you think it got to be so *orange,* man?"

"You got a point there. They say that shit causes cancer."

"I heard *that*."

I rounded a corner and cut through an alley on the way to my car. The line stretched halfway down the block, the usual tattered bums and drunks mixing with old people whose social security checks would be exhausted long before the next ones arrived. Breadlines. My parents used to tell me about them.

There were some unfamiliar faces, too: a woman with three children at her side, all dressed in crisp, clean clothes. The mother's tight-lipped expression suggested that this was a new experience for her. I'm not one of *them*, she seemed to be saying. Things are just a little tough for us right now.

I passed the end of the line and continued down the alley, approaching an entranceway. Somebody stood in the shadows. I pulled even with him and kept going. I was just past when he broke into the light behind me. I walked on, sneaking a look over my shoulder. Two steps back was Geraghty.

15

I stared straight ahead and kept walking, trying not to speed up too obviously. I could scream. People would hear. But what would he do? A normal man might run away, but Geraghty was not a normal man. So I kept on walking.

Geraghty stayed two paces back, synchronizing his footsteps with mine. Left foot, right foot, left foot, right foot. What a goddamn fascinating game. My heart was keeping time. The alley was coming to an end—right into another alley. A busy street was at least a block away. Turn left—or right?

I turned right. Bad move. This alley is deserted. Warehouses are sealed, gates are locked. Geraghty turned, too. I picked up my pace and so did he. He could close the distance with a lunge. The nerves in my back tensed up. Any second now, a hand on my shoulder. Left, right, left, right. Be cool. We're just out for a stroll. Why, there's the end of the alley up ahead, and a street with people and cars. How interesting. Let's check it out.

The street was two hundred feet away. I kept the pace, arms swinging loosely at my side, just like they tell you to do in self-defense class. Each step brought me three feet closer. Could I make it now if I ran? I had to try. Just a couple steps more. Left, right, left. Now *run*.

I burst blindly toward the street, arms and legs pumping, not even breathing. Blood roaring in my ears as I sprinted down the alley. It won't end, it just keeps going, the street's so far away. . . . He was running too, I felt him, his breath on my neck. He had me, grabbing my hair. I swatted him away and shot ahead. He struck again and held fast to my hair, snapping my head back. I stumbled. My palm scraped the ground. I pushed against it and kept my balance. Shook my head wildly and broke his grip. Surged forward, flying now, waiting for that hand again—then smacked into somebody and we crumpled to the ground.

"Ow! Sweet Jesus!" a man cried out.

I was lying on top of him. He was dressed in a wrinkled and dirty suit, and he smelled like—he smelled bad. I rolled onto the sidewalk and leaned on an elbow. Pain was blasting through my ribs; my breath was coming in jagged gasps.

"Oh no, oh no, oh no. . . ." The man was grabbing at his leg. "That was my *bad* one, it's twisted up now, it's hurtin' me . . . oh, Jesus. What was you *doin'*, woman? You plowed right into me!"

"Sorry," I panted, clutching my side. People were starting to gather. I decided that nothing new was broken. Somebody held out a hand and pulled me up. Somebody else asked if I was all right and offered to phone an ambulance; I said no thanks. The bum I'd hit was standing, too. "She plowed right into me!" he was saying to anyone who would listen. "Oooh," someone else said. "Girl be tumblin'!" I was looking around for that nightmarish face. But the alley was empty. The man with the shock-white crew cut was gone.

Needing a place to catch my breath and clean up, I limped two blocks to The Wayside. It was nearly four in the afternoon, and the street people were jockeying for a place in line outside. Time to sign up for beds. Generally there were twice as many applicants as there were beds, and the weaker men were often muscled into giving up their places in line. Deciding where you're going to sleep that night occupies the better part of your day South of Market. A foghorn sounded. It was a damp night coming.

107

Two minutes to four. The men squatting on the sidewalk stood up, unfolding their bodies with difficulty. Cigarettes were stubbed out, caps screwed back on bottles. Everybody moved a little closer.

Keys rattled behind the door; seconds later it was opened by Michael Sloane. The bums surged forward. "Hold it, now hold it!" Michael called out, making room to prop the door. "Take it easy, people, and don't crowd!"

The line moved, each man entering the foyer and giving his name to the woman seated at a card table. Having been checked against a list of undesirables, he then received a piece of colored paper and was passed on to a burly bouncer who frisked for weapons and let him through. The process would be repeated until all of the beds were assigned. The dozens of disappointed souls would then head off to another shelter or church, swapping rumors about the most promising possibilities. Others would start looking for a suitable doorway, or a good piece of cardboard.

I caught Michael's eye, and he motioned me in past the crowd. "My God," he said, staring at my grotesque appearance.

I sat in Michael's office while he went to get some bandages. Amazingly, my new injuries were nothing serious—bloody knee, scraped palm, and stiff neck. The pain was no worse, which is to say it was intense. Only my brain was numb. Less than half an hour had passed since my run-in with Geraghty, and I was still in shock. I just stared at the pastoral pictures on the wall. Through the bedlam came the sound of Early Times's piano. He was belting it out.

> Down in New Orleans where everything's fine,
> All of those cats just drinkin' that wine.
> Drinkin' that mess to their delight,
> And when they get high they start singin' all night.
>
> Drinkin' wine, spo-dee-o-dee, drinkin' wine,
> Wine, spo-dee-o-dee drinkin' wine,
> Wine, spo-dee-o-dee drinkin' wine,
> Pass that bottle to me.

Michael returned with a basin, knelt before me, and began dabbing at my knee with a wet washcloth. "As Marlene Dietrich said to Orson Welles in *Touch of Evil*, 'You a mess, honey.'"

"I've been told that," I said.

"It bears repeating. What'd you get yourself into this time?"

"I wish I knew." I started to laugh, but the pain in my ribs put a stop to that. "It was this guy who's been following Harry Cremmins around. Gerald Geraghty is his name. At least he *was* following Cremmins. Now he seems to be following me."

"Don't you think you'd better tell the police about this?"

"I don't know. I guess so. It's just that I seem to be getting close to something. Putting Geraghty in jail could be a mistake. Besides, what would I say? Nobody saw anything. And I hate to go crying to the cops."

"Since when did you start caring what cops think about you?" Michael wrung out some of my blood into the basin and tore open a Band-Aid.

"It's my job to care. I've made a career out of striking fear into the hearts of our city's finest. Unfortunately I appear to have lost that advantage when I left the P.D.'s."

"Whose fault is that?"

"Don't start."

"Sorry."

> Wine, spo-dee-o-dee drinkin' wine,
> Wine, spo-dee-o-dee drinkin' wine,
> Pass that bottle to me.

A couple of bums in the next room were making a feeble effort to sing along, yelling out "Wine!" every time E.T. reached the chorus.

"Michael, I will make you a deal."

He applied the Band-Aid tightly, smoothing it over my knee. "Shoot."

"Understand, this doesn't mean I'm working for you or anything—"

"Whatever you say."

"—but if you help me on this Tuttle murder, like you said you would, I'll try to find out who's setting you up on the development thing. To tell you the truth, I'm stuck. I need to know who Tuttle was spying on, all the places he hung out. All I've got is a notebook that's in some kind of code, and he didn't leave me his secret decoder ring. Meanwhile, I'll see what I can come up with on Malakis."

Michael's hand rested on my knee. "I'm starting to wonder whether you should be involved in this at all."

Again I tried to laugh; again my ribs hit back. *Starting* to wonder?"

My hand had landed on his. I felt safe in that office, a haven from the crazies, and I didn't want to leave.

"I'm not kidding," said Michael. "Look where it's got you. Can't walk down the street anymore without some psycho crawling up out of the sewer."

He was right. I had lost that magic shield that protected me as a public defender. I wasn't invisible anymore.

"So what?" I said. "Are you suggesting that I can't do the job?"

"I'm only saying that—"

"'A woman has a tougher time on the street just by virtue of her sex, and maybe she ought to consider not doing certain kinds of dangerous work,' et cetera, et cetera." This was an old argument between us that got revived from time to time.

"All right," Michael said. "You're hired again."

"That's not what I meant. I said I'll work *with* you, not *for* you."

"What the hell is the difference?"

"For you, none. But it makes a difference to me."

"Then have it your way. We're partners."

I didn't like the sound of that either.

"I don't get it," Michael said. "What's the problem?"

"Want me to be honest?"

"Of course."

"I think you want to find Tommy so you can make him your performing flea."

"Spare me."

"Well, don't you?"

He sighed. "Somebody just tried to kill you. Sherman Tuttle was carved up in a trash can. And if Tommy Malakis is alive, we'd like to keep him in one piece. The rest of it's bullshit, okay?"

Michael squeezed my hand in earnest. It was more than a friendly gesture. I returned the pressure, then slowly took the hand away.

> I've got a nickel if you've got a dime,
> Let's get together and buy some wine.
> Some buy the fifth, some buy the quart,
> When you buy blackberry you doin' things smart.

> Wine, spo-dee-o-dee, drinkin' wine . . .

"Wine!" the bums sang out.

"So I help you with the Tuttle case, and you help me find Malakis."

"That's right," I said.

Michael sighed. "What makes you so ornery, Thorpe? The Irish or the Italian?"

"The Catholic. Is it a deal?"

"Deal."

> . . . Give that bottle to me!

That night I double-locked the doors of my house. Reliving the scene in the alley gave me the sweats. Geraghty *was* coming after me now, for whatever reason. Everyone involved with Malakis was fair game for this madman.

To make myself feel better, I made a peanut butter and mayonnaise sandwich and vowed to wrestle with Tuttle's notebook for the rest of the evening. It was maddening. Seven colors times twenty-six letters: a staggering number of possibilities. By now I had acquired the necessary colored pens, and I went to work, counting up the green S's and the red M's and the orange W's. I tried standard cryptography again, placing E's over the combinations that seemed to occur the most times, then T's, then the rest of the vowels, ad nauseam. Impossible. I was certain that the key changed with every page and new set of numbers. Nothing emerged from the nonsense. Of course not, I thought, he was crazy. He made up his own language, that's what crazy people do.

I scolded myself for this attitude and tried another section of the book. Pages . . . dates . . . maybe they contained the key within themselves. But I didn't see how.

It was getting late. Before I knew it I was reaching for a phone book, and not as a clue to Tuttle's cipher. I had already tried that. I was looking at the W's: Whale, Whallen, Whallman. No Whaley. Try Oakland. Some Whaleys there, but no Emma. Try Marin County. I don't have that book. Try San Mateo. Try Palo Alto.

There she was, Emma Whaley, living on Forest Street in Palo Alto.

16

It was two days before I got up the resolve to drive to Palo Alto. Two days closer to Michael Sloane's big meeting with the developers, but what did I care? I needed the extra time. I had intended to follow up the Emma Whaley lead right away. But when I got out of bed the next morning, I was seized by inaction, contradictory as that might sound. My muscles felt encased in lead. The encounter with Geraghty was only part of the reason. I had been having these deadening spells with regularity over the past year, although it was some time since the last one, well before Sherman Tuttle had appeared in my office nearly two weeks ago. I had learned to ride them out, knowing that they would pass in a day or so. So I unplugged the phone and stayed in the house, tinkering with the jukeboxes for a while, but mostly just sitting in a comfortable chair, drinking tea and staring at that jumble of colored letters. Watching summer fade.

On Friday the spell dissipated, and I was out the door by nine o'clock. It was good to get away from the city. Driving down the peninsula, I decided to spend the weekend with Sara Ludlow in Santa Rosa.

Emma Whaley's house was a one-story stucco affair obscured by a gnarled oak tree. Through the branches peeked decorative shutters and an empty flower box running the length of the living room window. A vine-covered trellis screened in most of the porch. The lawn was scattered with crackling orange leaves.

Palo Alto, about fifty miles south of San Francisco, is an old town, a university town, with tree-lined streets and a suburban atmosphere. I felt that I knew Emma a bit by understanding the transition she had gone through. From owner of a skid row hotel to a lovely little home light years away from the winos, pimps, and junkies: she had found a way out. It was life with the edges sanded down, the horrors muted.

I rang the doorbell. She was a long time in answering, and she cracked the door a few inches to get a look at me before opening it wide.

"Emma Whaley?"

"Yes, that's me." Her voice was friendly, belying the impression of seclusion that her house gave off. She was on the heavy side, in her sixties, gray hair neatly in place, as if she slept in a hair net. Most of the lines in her face were centered around the mouth. No makeup; the ruddiness in her cheeks was genuine. She wore a floral blouse, calf-length linen skirt, and fluffy pink slippers.

"I'm Cassandra Thorpe, a private . . . an investigator from the public defender's office in San Francisco. We're working on a case that involves the Doyle Hotel, and I'd like to ask you a question or two about it. Just for the sake of background." Just the facts, ma'am.

"Yes?" Her immobility didn't appear to be a sign of unfriendliness; she was still smiling. But she wasn't moving.

"May I come in for a moment?"

Surprised at her own inhospitality, she moved aside. "Of course."

A short hallway split into the kitchen on the right, living room on the left. She gestured to the left, and followed me in.

The day wasn't cold, but she had a small fire going. The dustless room was furnished with things that were old but clean—clawfoot chairs and a sofa protected by lace antimacassars, a tray with a cut-glass decanter and cordial glasses, TV set on a shaky wire stand with wheels. The walls were olive green, and so was the worn shag rug. It was like going to Grandma's house, but something was missing.

Mrs. Whaley settled into her favorite chair—it had a matching footstool and a thick romance novel lay open on it—while I took a seat at the edge of the couch. Sunlight was blocked by the big oak tree, and her chair was bathed in the glow of a pole lamp. The air was heavy and stale. The setting reminded me of the time that my grandmother took me to visit the Carmelite nuns. I was eight years old, and awed by their reclusive lives. I shook the hand of one of them through a wooden connecting drawer, set into the wall that separated us.

She waited for me to start, wearing that fixed smile that I was fast becoming used to.

"Well . . . you used to own the Doyle, right?" I asked.

"Many years ago I did, yes."

"And your husband?"

"I'm a widow." The words seemed to come out with a slight edge, but it might have been my imagination. So much for finding Virgil Whaley.

"No, I mean back then," I said. "You both owned it?"

"It was in both our names."

"When you sold it?"

The smile vanished for the first time. Or maybe the wrinkles around the mouth had only suggested a smile, because I hadn't actually seen it disappear.

"What was it you wanted, dear?" she asked in a perfectly civil tone.

"Well, Mrs. Whaley, I'd very much like to know who bought the hotel from you. We need to trace its history for a client . . . actually we're trying to establish the ownership of several buildings in that area." I sketched in a few details about the hotel development and, without mentioning Tommy Malakis, suggested that the present-day developers were suspected of wrongdoing. Most of it was the truth, but that didn't stop me from feeling disgust over lying to an old lady.

115

"I'm sorry," she said, "but I can't remember the name off-hand . . . it was a real estate company, I think. I haven't seen the papers for a very long time. . . ."

"Would your husband have kept any records, do you think?"

"My husband died just before the hotel was sold. I was the one who sold it. I'm sorry I can't remember any more than that."

"Then you bought this house with the money from the sale of the hotel?"

"That's right." Mrs. Whaley's voice was hardening.

"Could you tell me . . . exactly when your husband passed away?"

"I don't see how that can help you." The interview was fast coming to an end. Any vestige of friendliness had vanished; Emma was gripping the arms of her chair as if she were peeling down the runway in a jet. I couldn't blame her for being defensive. A husband who ran off with another woman and left her in possession of a rat-infested hotel . . . Better to say he was dead, especially if she had loved him.

"It would make it possible to trace ownership of the Doyle a little further back. If you could say exactly how long you and your husband owned the Doyle . . ."

She was getting out of her chair. These weren't the slow, deliberate moves of the grandmother who had greeted me at the door. "I'm very tired," she announced. "You'll have to go."

Again, that look of fear—just like on the face of Harry Cremmins, with the same feeble defensiveness. Until now I had favored Cremmins as the arsonist. But what kind of man was Virgil Whaley? He had tried to buy the Leeward Inn, and shortly thereafter the bar went up in flames. Then he ran off, "with another woman."

Emma Whaley followed me to the door, shuffling along in her slippers on the drab olive carpet. Suddenly I realized, as the front door opened and fresh air came wafting in, what was missing from her bland little house. There wasn't a framed picture or photograph to be seen—not on the wall, not on the mantel, nowhere. In the peaceful life of an old lady who could be anybody's grandmother, not a single memory was on display.

I took an elbow in the ribs—on my good side, thank God—and a shove from behind. Then somebody stepped on my foot. I ducked to avoid an object flying through the air. It was a pack of cigarettes, and it was caught by a man standing behind me. He stared as he tapped out a single smoke and placed it between his lips.

The noise was deafening, twenty men shouting at the top of their lungs in an L-shaped room whose longer end was only nine feet long. I was wedged into a holding cell at the Hall of Justice. Every courtroom has one, where prisoners are kept while waiting to be arraigned, tried, or sentenced. Returning from Palo Alto, I had made the mistake of stopping by Sonia's office just before lunchtime. Instantly I was recruited to help out on a trial that was about to begin. Her client was the man accused of driving around a stereo store. Because she was busy in the judge's chambers, it was my task to convince him to take the plea bargain that had been worked out between Sonia and the D.A. So there I was again, stuck at the Hall of Justice on a Friday.

The beating that I was taking in the cell was unintended; just standing there for five minutes in that jostling pack of unwashed bodies and thick smoke was enough to turn anyone black and blue. Few of the men could refrain from some reasonably graphic description of what they would do to me if the two of us could only be alone for a few minutes. Somewhere out in the hall was a bailiff with the key. Bailiffs are a fun-loving sort, and on occasion they like to break for coffee just about the time that a P.D. is knocking on the door of the holding cell to be let out.

Trying my best to protect my battered body, I squeezed through the sea of orange jumpsuits to the black man slumped on a bench, coolly smoking a cigarette.

"Raymond Lutrell?" I shouted, barely able to hear my own voice.

The man raised an eyelid.

117

"I'm here on behalf of Miss Baine, your public defender. You're about to go in to trial, and she asked me to cover a couple of things for her."

Lutrell grinned obscenely. "You just as pretty as the other bitch," he said. "Even though you white."

"It's about the D.A.'s offer. I'll lay it out for you as clearly as I can—"

"Yeah, go ahead and *lay it out*." He grinned again. Just make it through this one interview, I thought. You don't have to put up with this crap anymore.

"Right now there's two counts against you," I continued. "One for receiving, one for auto burg, and a one-year prior. So your maximum exposure is four years. Understand?"

"I ain't spending time in no joint."

"So here's the offer. Plead to the auto burg. Take probation. That's three years' state prison time suspended, three years' probation, and six months in the county jail. If you screw up in that three years—if you blow your nose wrong or look cross-eyed at a cop—it's another bus ride to the joint. Now your second option is the low term of sixteen months. . . ."

Months had passed since I'd made The Speech, but it still came automatically. There was a time when I'd rattle it off five times a day or more. Trying to lay out the "options" for a guy who doesn't begin to comprehend the system of which he's a part, and hates my guts for what he's doing to himself. No wonder the words came out without having to think.

A man shackled at the wrists and ankles stumbled into my bruised arm. I cried out. "Hey," said Lutrell, "you look like you hurtin'. What's the matter, you get in a fight with your old man?" He laughed.

"You listening, or not?"

"Not. I ain't talkin' to nobody till you get me somethin' better. I know that judge ain't gonna give me no full time. Maybe I won't even have to *do* time. You get me a real lawyer."

I moved in close, ignoring the stink and the sweat. "Listen to me. You've been around too long to believe that bullshit. But go ahead if you want to. It's not me who's doing the four years. I don't give a shit. Got it?"

That, too, was rehearsed. I pulled it out, with minor variations, every time a client started acting up—which was one out of every three clients. The shock effect of a woman talking back usually shaped them up. The only difference now was in my feelings. Once the speech was bluster. Now there was real anger in it. I was trying to help this client at the same time I was thinking, Go rot.

"Okay," Lutrell finally said. "Tell her I'll take the deal." His pride wouldn't allow him to look at me again.

I nodded and stood up, enduring the familiar discomfort of stretching. "They'll call you out in a few minutes," I said, and started to the door.

At first the pressure felt like another inadvertent collision—just a hand on my elbow. I tried to shake it off. The pressure increased. All of a sudden my bruised arm was being yanked back and twisted until it was about to pop out of the socket. Another arm grabbed me, digging into my broken ribs. Pain was lacerating my body. He yanked me to him and held me for a long time.

Everybody was watching. No one was going to help. Some were trying not to look. Even in that tiny space they had managed to draw away.

I had been too shocked to cry out. Now, as I started to, the man squeezed me even harder. The arm rose to my throat, cutting off my air. The stink was horrifying. Lips brushed my ear. His breath was hot and stale.

"Word is out," the man whispered. "Remember Sherman Tuttle?"

I could only rasp out a cough.

"You got something of his. Louis Boudeaux wants it. He wants *all* of it, bitch. In twenty-four hours. He'll be waiting."

Releasing his grip, he shoved me into a couple of jumpsuits. They caught me and helped me to my feet. I turned to face my attacker. Twenty men stared back, all with the same blank expression. Any one of them could have done it.

I staggered to the door and started pounding for the bailiff to come and let me out. Pounded away, leaning against that heavy door, while the men in the room watched in total silence. The bailiff, where the hell was he?

Finally the son of a bitch came to take me away.

17

Arm steady. Hold your breath. Concentrate. Don't aim down on the target, bring the gun *up*. Relax. Squeeze the trigger.

I missed.

The earmuffs deadened the sound of the explosion, and the tiny weapon didn't have much of a kick to it. It was something independent of me, firing by itself as I watched through a window.

Still too nervous. Try again. A cardboard silhouette of a man hung on a wire 100 feet away, rocking in the breeze. I readjusted the earmuffs, stretched my neck and shoulders, planted my feet, and raised the gun.

Elroy's Saturday-night special had sat in my purse ever since Sherman Tuttle's murder. It felt comfortable there. Taking it out of the file cabinet had been a semiconscious act, like packing a security blanket. Now my possession of the weapon was deliberate. What little control I had over the situation was slipping away. Santa Rosa could wait another week; I had to learn how to fire a gun.

The outdoor range at Lake Merced, in the southwestern corner of the city, had a sign over the entrance: 56 YEARS OF MAINTAINING AN ACCIDENT-FREE FACILITY. Maybe I'll be the one to break the record, I thought.

Fire. A corner of the cardboard dissolved into dust. Concentration was the hardest part. Thoughts kept muscling in, shouting while I aimed. One name kept coming around: Louis Boudeaux. The city's most notorious heroin kingpin. A black man from the streets of New Orleans, Boudeaux had come to San Francisco six years ago and promptly wrested control of the dope trade away from the white businessmen. He used eight-year-olds from the projects as lookouts, and teenagers as lieutenants. Boudeaux's army was a rigid hierarchy with plenty of chances for advancement. Sometimes he would drive through the neighborhood and toss hundred-dollar bills to the kids. Loyalty was secured through a combination of generosity and terror. Dozens went to prison to protect his good name. Boudeaux's reach was very, very long.

Now he was reaching for me—or, to be more accurate, for Sherman Tuttle. Somewhere in that coded diary was information that "belonged" to Boudeaux. Michael Sloane wasn't the only one who had been pestered by Tuttle. If you hung around South of Market long enough, equipped with enough felt pens, charts, and the proper sense of paranoia, you were bound to stumble onto something real. Tuttle had charted the life of the wrong man.

Fire. Another clean miss. Reload.

I remembered the dope dealer whom Michael had unceremoniously booted out of The Wayside the night I showed up with Harry Cremmins. It wasn't the first time that Michael had disrupted local commerce in the dining room. Suppose it was Boudeaux who steered Sherman Tuttle to The Wayside in the first place. Or maybe Boudeaux had an interest in Sunrise City, and wanted to discredit Michael as a spokesman for the neighborhood. But Tuttle, being not of sound mind, was undependable. He would have started spying on Boudeaux, too. And gotten himself murdered.

Then there was Tommy Malakis, and another mass of maybes. Maybe Gerald Geraghty was out for revenge for the death of a friend in the Leeward Inn fire. Maybe Virgil Whaley burned it down. Maybe Harry Cremmins really believed that a treasure was buried in the parking lot.

At the center of it all was a frightened old man who made the mistake of publicly announcing his resurrection. I thought of Tommy hiding out somewhere, looking for a "safeplace" in a world of Geraghtys and Boudeauxs and Whaleys. The enemy seemed too powerful.

The wording of his note was strange, come to think of it. I AM COMING BACK. TELL NO ONE. I WILL BE COMING BACK FOR MY TRESHURE. HELP ME. *I am coming back*, not *I am back*. Of course, I thought—he hadn't arrived yet, at least not at the time the note was delivered. If his words were to be taken literally, then someone must have acted for him. A messenger. An advance guard.

Harry Cremmins?

I squeezed off two more shots. One pierced the cardboard just two inches from the edge of the bull's-eye, the silhouette's heart. It seemed unlikely. In the classic manner of the alcoholic, Cremmins appeared to blame Malakis for everything that had happened to him. Why do Tommy a favor? Cremmins saw the treasure as payment for his years of suffering. But there was no treasure. And if Cremmins wasn't the messenger, who was? My head hurt.

The firing was becoming more rhythmic as I began to relax. I had to find Cremmins again. He was my only lead—and the only witness to the presence of Virgil Whaley at the Leeward. Maybe. Aim and fire. Malakis and Geraghty. Tuttle and Boudeaux. Weak and strong, prey and predator. Aim and fire. The world seemed divided up that way, and I was in the middle. I'm not up to it, I thought. Fire. I'm not strong enough. Let somebody else do it. Fire.

Click. I snapped out of the trance, reaching into my pocket for more ammunition. Empty. I looked at the cardboard for the first time. It was riddled with bullet holes. Somebody had gotten a little carried away.

I took away my shot-up slab of cardboard as a souvenir and drove out to the Hooverville under the freeway. A crowd was clustered around the rusting Muni bus, arguing with a man in a shabby bus inspector's uniform. A couple of the bums were banging on the bus and yelling. The hapless Muni man was blocking the door.

"We're not in the business of renting out mobile homes," the man was saying. "The bus was intended as temporary shelter—"

"Temporary my ass!" said a man in a tattered army jacket and stocking cap. "How'd you like me telling you *your* house was tempo-rary, sucker?"

"Yeah," another one chimed in. "Where you gonna put us anyway?"

"That's not my department," said the Muni man, raising his hands. "I work for the Municipal Railway, and all they told me was, 'Go get that bus.' A third of our fleet is broken down, and we need every vehicle we've got!"

"But we *like* it here," said a man whose jacket was covered with different colors of electrician's tape. "We fixed it up and everything."

"We like ridin' on it!" someone else cried out.

Scanning the crowd for Cremmins, I eased past the bums to the man in the doorway. He was tall and stringy, beyond retirement age. He saw me coming and groaned.

"And who are you? A reporter? Somebody from Social Services? I'm under orders here. You got any problems with that, call the mayor's office or something, I don't know, but let me do my job."

"I'm looking for a man. He was living on this bus three days ago. I'd like to check, if you don't mind."

"I'm not supposed to let anyone—" But I was already inside.

The bus was even dirtier than before, thick with the smell of rot. Trash choked the aisles; seats were piled high with blankets, newspapers, and tin cans. The inhabitants had wasted no time in staking out their territory.

Seat by seat I checked for signs of a man buried beneath garbage. "Are you happy now?" the Muni man called out from the doorway. "You see what these . . . bums have done to my bus?" The back seat was vacant. I would search the shelters again, but I knew I wouldn't find Cremmins. After all, I was the one who had scared him away by accusing him of burning down the Leeward. He was my only link to Malakis. Now he was running.

"Will you get back . . ." the Muni man was saying to the

crowd as I stepped down. Using me as a diversion, he lunged for the lever beside the steering wheel. The door exhaled and swung shut, trapping the hand of the man with the stocking cap. "Hey!" he cried, yanking at it as the bus's engine roared into life.

His hand was caught in the rubber door seals. He planted his foot on the step and tugged. I grabbed his wrist. The bus started to move. "Stop!" the bums were crying as we struggled to keep our footing. The trapped man teetered on the step, then slipped. I fell too, and now his arm was supporting the weight of my body. "Son of a bitch!" he growled. The bus was picking up speed, the bums jogging alongside. I tried to regain my footing but got tangled in the man's legs. We were dragging through the mud, we must have looked ridiculous, but all I knew was the pain tearing up my arm. It's going, I thought. It's coming right off at the goddamn socket. "Let *go* of me!" the man screamed. Suddenly his hand popped free of the door seals and we went sprawling. With a final kick, the bus lurched off down the street, belching smoke and dust.

I got up and dusted myself off, ignoring the reignited fire in my ribs and arm, and turned to the crowd of staring bums. "Anybody here know Harry Cremmins?" I said between gasps. But all I saw through watery eyes was a sea of shaking heads.

I retreated to my office. I could no longer afford a leisurely investigation. Cremmins was in danger, maybe even dead. Malakis had underestimated the perils of returning to San Francisco. For all I knew Michael might give up on him and milk the "treasure" story anyway, just for the publicity. The developers' meeting was only four days away. Then there was my own neck to worry about—Louis Boudeaux was coming for me.

Chances were that Cremmins had left the city. He seemed frightened enough. Where had he come from? *Ukiah can get out a paper that don't make your hands dirty,* he said. That was a town about two and a half hours north of San Francisco, in Mendocino County. Maybe Malakis was up there, too. It was an area with large sections of forest and rural communities that might take weeks to comb. I needed a starting point.

On my way back to the office I had stopped at the Northern California Service League to pick up a list of all shelters and halfway houses north of San Francisco. Now I was looking at the ones around Ukiah. There was a drug rehab center, run by one of those groups that shave your head and use you as slave labor while you sweat out your addictions. A Salvation Army outpost. And a couple of churches with cots in the basement. Not much of a safety net— but then bums were supposed to stay in the big cities, where they belonged. The rural areas were reserved for mass murderers and guys who turned cheerleaders into sex slaves.

I started making some phone calls, posing as an investigator with the public defender's office. Nobody knew a Tommy Malakis, and I didn't have a description that could be conveyed over the telephone. As for Harry Cremmins, no one place had heard of him. They all had.

Cremmins was the town drunk, the local embarrassment, the bogeyman who would come for the kids who didn't do their homework or eat their lima beans. For ten years he had staggered down the streets of Ukiah, numbed by the fruits of the wine country. Then one day he left—and took a piece of Ukiah with him.

"He stole money from the high school band fund," said Rachel Rasmussen, pastor of the Lutheran Church of the Holy Testament. "Is he in San Francisco? He really should be arrested. We're short our goal, thanks to him."

That must be the hundred dollars that Cremmins had managed to hold on to for five minutes upon arriving in San Francisco. I thanked Pastor Rasmussen and said I would see her the following day, between services.

Being a petty thief, Cremmins wasn't likely to return to Ukiah in the near future. But it was worth the trip anyway. If I could trace his life in the town, it might lead me to Malakis. And I could stop off in Santa Rosa and see Sara

Ludlow. I called to ask her if it was okay. She would be overjoyed to see me, she said.

There were, of course, other considerations. An arm around my throat, a voice in my ear. Louis Boudeaux's twenty-four hours were up. I went down the dark stairs.

Gee, I thought. This investigation business is easy.

18

The alley was full of shadows that could hold Geraghty—or worse. I walked through the twilight with unnatural speed, resisting the temptation to look over my shoulder every three steps. A wino shambled by and brushed against me; it felt like an electric shock. Dark doorways loomed on every side. From somewhere came the rhythmic squeal of metal scraping metal. I passed a tiny "children's" park. A derelict was slumped in a swing, gently rocking. A TV set blared from an open window.

One of the cars in the parking lot was a dark-colored van with smoked windows. It looked familiar—a deep purple airbrushed onto black, an idyllic mountainscape inked on the side. The flawless paint job glittered in the dusk. What kind of car was blocking the alley the day I was attacked? I couldn't remember.

I unlocked my car door with trembling hands, dove inside, and locked it. Not before glancing at the back seat, of course. I slid out of the lot, trying not to floor the accelerator. The neighborhood was giving me the shakes like never before.

Reaching my house safely was another problem. Because of the jukeboxes I couldn't use the garage, and the space I found after twenty minutes of frying my clutch on the hillside was three dark blocks away. Again I had that feeling of being pursued. I'm getting to be as bad as Sherman Tuttle, I thought. And look what happened to him.

I told myself to knock it off, and marched up to the house. First I wanted to check that Sherman's notebook was safe in its hiding place—one of the jukeboxes in the garage—and I decided to enter there. It wasn't until I got the key in the lock that I heard the music. Coming from inside. Little Richard, belting out "Lucille."

I slid the key out. The only light was coming through the cracks of the garage door. I went around to the side, through the gate, and to the kitchen entrance.

Here the music was barely audible. Slipping into the kitchen, I set my purse on the counter and withdrew the gun. I stood before the door to the garage, rock still.

"Luceeeee-ille!" someone was screaming along with the music, drowning out Little Richard. "Luceeeeeeeee-ille!" The record was fading, and the now-familiar voice yelled her name one more time, horribly out of tune. I shoved the door open.

Eddie jumped back, colliding with one of the jukeboxes. "God damn!" he cried. "Was that necessary?" His injuries, like mine, had settled into nasty purplish blotches.

"What are you doing in my house?" I looked at the gun in my hand. My knuckles were chalk white.

"It's mine too, you know," he said, searching for that air of dignity he would never find.

"Not anymore."

"Yeah, well what about these jukes? Who brought them here, huh?"

"And who almost went to jail because he couldn't afford to pay for them and didn't know a damned thing about fixing them? Now will you tell me what you're doing here, or do I have to throw you out?"

Eddie shook his head. "You've changed, Cass, you realize that? You used to be a much nicer person. Now you only talk to me when you want something, and even then it's most of the time to get me tangled up in some—"

"Eddie."

"Okay, okay. I just need like a place to hide . . . to lay low for a while. I can't seem to shake these jerks who want my pictures. Maybe you shoulda kept them, I don't know. Anyway, they're asking all over town, they say they're gonna twist my legs off if they find me . . . big shots. So I'm thinking you could like put me up for a few nights, just till things blow over. Man, I'm really gonna nail those assholes."

"Come out of the garage." The cramp in my hand had relaxed. Right now any company was welcome. "Under normal circumstances I'd tell you to take a hike, but it just so happens that I have to leave town for a few days. So you can stay."

"All right, Cass!" Eddie threw his arms around me. I was going to shrug him off, but he broke first. He was staring at the weapon in my hand.

"Hey. Whatcha got there?"

"A gun."

"Yeah . . . I didn't know you carried a . . . you were gonna . . ." He shuddered. "Who the hell did you think I was?"

"I have to pack," I said, and left him in the kitchen.

I reached Santa Rosa about midnight. The day's heat still hung in the air, promising another week of ninety-degree temperatures. Real summer weather. I hugged Sara for a long time, took five minutes to explain my appearance, then excused myself and went to bed. I was looking forward to a night's peaceful sleep.

I was out of luck. It was a fitful, endless night, disturbed by psychopaths in alleys, people on fire, knives slashing at the air. Finally the dream came, with brutal clarity.

I am kneeling at a church altar, surrounded by people. An organ drones. My mother kneels beside me, crying. Years since I've been inside. . . . Everything has an oppressive, late-morning feel to it. My limbs feel drugged. The stained glass blazes with sunlight, splashing color on the walls. I keep hearing the words: *The body of Christ. Amen. The body of Christ. Amen. . . .*

Then it is my turn. The priest stands before me in purple

vestments, holding the chalice aloft. An altar boy slips the polished plate under my chin. The diaphanous wafer catches the colored light. Hard to see in the glare. My knees and back ache. I open my mouth. *The body of Christ*, the priest says softly.

This is a test, I think. A test of control. Everybody's watching. I accept the Host. It rests on my tongue like cardboard. I forgot to say *Amen*. My knees begin to shake. It's almost over. They're watching. . . .

But my legs give out, I fall to the floor, the plate goes flying, and suddenly I lie helpless at the priest's feet, the tears pouring forth in waves. My body shakes like an epileptic's. People are clustering round, murmuring to each other, and someone places a hand on my shoulder, saying *There, there*. But I can't stop. Two men take my arms, raise me to my feet, and lead me away. They all watch me go; I am still sobbing violently, shamelessly. A grown woman, out of control. The organ drones on.

I was grateful for morning.

The big sign on the high school lawn was shaped like a thermometer, marked in dollars instead of degrees. The mercury reached to the top. SEND OUR BAND TO DENMARK, the sign read. INTERNATIONAL HIGH SCHOOL MARCHING BAND COMPETITION. Next door the congregation was filing out of the Lutheran church, a white clapboard building with a steeple, and stained-glass lancets along the sides.

"They had the money," said Pastor Rasmussen, a tall, Nordic-looking woman in a white surplice. "Then *he* came along, and set us back another two weeks. It makes you wonder about people, doesn't it?"

Yes, I thought. Stealing a hundred dollars from the marching band really is a hideous crime. "How did he break into the school?"

"It wasn't exactly a break-in. We were painting the church that weekend, so the cots were moved over to the gymnasium."

"And Cremmins went with them?"

"About a dozen people, actually. They were supposed to

stay in the gym, but he started wandering the hallways. A janitor saw him near the principal's office. A few minutes later the money was gone. There was a fund-raiser the night before and nobody had bothered to put it in the safe."

"What happened to Cremmins?"

"We assume he took the bus to San Francisco. Bert Hansen over at the station remembers him buying a ticket. We haven't seen him since." She shook her head. "For ten years the merchants tried to get rid of the man. Now this."

We were walking back to the church. "What about the others sleeping there that night? Were they all regulars, too?"

"They come and go, but they're mostly the same out-of-work loggers and farmers. We have a lot of unemployment up here, you know. But nobody like Harry Cremmins. He never wanted to work. There was no sympathy for him."

Several members of the flock greeted Pastor Rasmussen on their way to the next service, dressed in pastels and patent leather pumps and Sunday suits. Everyone looked blissful. Not a very hospitable environment for someone like Tommy Malakis.

"If the theft was discovered so soon," I asked, "why didn't you stop Cremmins from getting away? If everybody knows him, I mean."

"There was a lot of confusion that day. An old man got hit by a bus at the station. We were too busy getting him to the hospital to think of anything else."

"You were helping? How come?"

"He'd just come to the church shelter, I mean the gym. Now that you mention it, *he* wasn't a regular. That was the first time I'd seen him."

"What was his name?"

We climbed the steps to the church entrance. "You know, we never asked. Not even when we sent his things to County General."

"They were left at the station?"

"No, at the gym. He left everything behind—jacket, sleeping bag, cigarettes. Which is funny because he'd

131

bought a ticket for that bus. I guess he didn't care about the stuff, it was awfully ratty anyway."

Bums care more for their possessions than anyone, no matter how "ratty." A sleeping bag and jacket are as valuable to a street person as platinum.

"How did he get hurt?"

"He stepped off the curb as the bus was pulling into the station. Why are you interested in this man? I thought you were looking for Harry Cremmins."

"He was taking the bus," I said, almost to myself.

"I told you, he *took* the bus."

"But if he had to go to the hospital—"

"I'm talking about Cremmins," Pastor Rasmussen said, growing impatient with me.

"Harry took *that* bus? The same one that hit the old man?"

"They only come three times a day. That was the last one."

Pastor Rasmussen turned her attention to the people coming up the steps. I peeked inside. It was an austere church, with stark white walls and hymnbooks arranged perfectly in the pews. Above the altar was a tortured Christ on the cross. It looked like any other Protestant church, but then I could never tell the difference between the sects.

"Do you want me to testify?" asked Pastor Rasmussen.

"Testify?" Were Lutherans like Baptists, singing gospel songs and talking in tongues?

"In court," she said. "When you prosecute."

From the look on my face, she knew I didn't comprehend.

"Isn't the district attorney going to pursue this? A hundred dollars may not be much by your standards, but it means something to the school."

"I'm not . . ." It wasn't worth explaining. People are always confusing public defenders with district attorneys. Even my mother did it, but that was probably wishful thinking on her part.

I thanked the pastor, and said I couldn't stay for the service.

*   *   *

Mendocino County General wasn't the liveliest place on a Sunday afternoon. It was a long time before they found someone who knew about the man who had been struck by a bus nearly two months ago. What little anyone there knew, that is—since they never learned his name. He was an amnesiac, a John Doe. For a week he had lain in bed, watching TV, receiving no visitors or phone calls. Then he was transferred.

"Transferred where?" I asked the hospital administrator, a harried nurse who would rather have been elsewhere.

She consulted a file. "Anderson Valley Clinic. Near Boonville. They take our overflow from time to time. He needed additional therapy. And we needed the bed."

The Anderson Valley lies between Highway 101 and the Mendocino coastline. The road connecting the two is one of the most beautiful in California. An hour of driving takes you through small towns, wineries, farms, apple orchards, lakes, evergreens, mountains, and fog-enshrouded redwoods, ending in cliffs overlooking the sea. Not a bad place to put a mental hospital, I thought. Maybe I should check in.

The lobby was done up in earth tones, with Navaho rugs and paintings from the Blue Chip Stamp catalogue. Muzak leaked from a ceiling speaker. The magazines on the coffee table were about wine, architecture, and crafts; not one carried news of the outside world. I was reading a Boonville paper about the strange local language called Boontling, invented by the natives in the late nineteenth century to exclude outsiders. Just like Sherman Tuttle, they had a secret code to describe everything from sex to baseball. And they say city people are weird, I thought.

"Keep the paper. Souvenir of the Anderson Valley."

Standing over me was a man in his forties with strands of gray through his immaculately brushed brown hair, and a healthy tan. He wore an expensive jogging suit, and a towel was wrapped around his neck.

"I mean it. Our patients help to put out the paper. I'm Dr. Barrett, director of the clinic."

"Cassandra Thorpe, Department of Social Services. I un-

133

derstand you had a John Doe here. A transfer from County General."

"You mean Max."

"He told you his name?"

"That's the only thing he's told us. In six weeks."

"He's still here, then."

"Not for long. We're going to have to release him soon. We need—"

"The bed, I know." Another product of deinstitutionalization, about to hit the streets. "May I see him?"

"You're his social worker?"

"Won't know till I see him."

Dr. Barrett seemed to want more information.

"We're holding some welfare checks," I said. "They may be his."

"Come on then."

We crossed the lawn of the ranch-style complex to another building. Only the droning of crickets broke the silence. The grounds were strangely deserted—or maybe I was thinking of those mammoth county facilities where nut cases wander the corridors goggling at visitors. This place seemed more like a rest home. I asked Dr. Barrett about it.

"Actually, that's a good analogy. Everyone's here voluntarily. They check in and check out whenever they want. We like to think of the clinic as a sanctuary, not a hospital. It's a beautiful setting, isn't it?"

"Hmm. What do you know about the accident?"

We had reached the building. "According to the report he just stepped in front of a bus for no apparent reason," he said.

"How badly was he hurt?"

"Nothing broken. Mild concussion, shock. The man's quite old, you know. And his mental state is questionable. At this point it's difficult to tell how much is the amnesia, and how much other problems. We can't keep him for more than another week or so."

Down a Muzak-filled hallway with the identical framed reproductions. We stopped before a closed door. "He doesn't have a lot to say," Dr. Barrett said. "I doubt you'll have

134

much luck communicating." He knocked and opened the door.

He was sitting in a wheelchair in a corner of the eight-by-twelve room, staring out the window. A bathrobe lay on the unmade bed. Atop a nightstand stood a plastic cup, an alarm clock, and a bus ticket. A pair of wingtips lay by the bed; loose change and a hairbrush were scattered on a dresser with broken knobs. A floral print hung on the wall. It looked as if he had just checked in.

"Max?" said Dr. Barrett. "Someone's here to see you."

The man in the wheelchair kept staring out the window. "Max," Dr. Barrett repeated. "You've got a visitor. All the way from San Francisco."

Like one of Hollywood Alice's game shows. "Cass has come all the way from San Francisco to be here today. . . ."

Max turned his head sharply. He was about seventy, with wisps of soft white hair atop a bald head. The eyes were buried in wrinkles, pupils invisible. The folds of his neck disappeared into a white short-sleeve dress shirt. His pants were pulled up to his chest. A blanket covered his lap. One shriveled hand held the Sunday comics page; the other was clenched in a fist.

"Well?" muttered Dr. Barrett.

"May I speak to him alone for a moment?"

Dr. Barrett shrugged and withdrew, closing the door behind him. I sensed he was still standing just outside.

Max watched the wall above my head with a bemused expression. His mouth was curved at the corners into a perpetual smile. We were sizing each other up.

"Hello, Tommy," I finally said.

No reaction, unless the smile turned up a bit more. "Tommy Malakis?" I asked.

The man waited for me to continue.

"Is that your name?"

Still no response. I should be more confident, I thought. After all, he just happened to show up in Ukiah the day Harry Cremmins decided to leave town in a hurry for the first time in ten years. In fact both of them were in a hurry. And they would have caught the same bus to San Francisco—if this old man hadn't stepped off the curb a little too early.

"I'm a friend of Michael Sloane, at The Wayside," I said. "Remember you wrote to him?"

Then he spoke. In a shaky voice, weaker even than the man appeared to be, with a slight accent that was impossible to pin down. "I am sorry," were his words.

"Sorry? For what? Tell me."

He was shaking his head, his face clouded with sadness. "I am sorry," he said again. "I don't know what you want."

Time to start pulling out the tricks. "Do you know Harry Cremmins?"

The head kept shaking. "I'll tell you who *I* am," I went on. "My name is Cassandra Thorpe. I'm here to help you get your treasure back. Remember the treasure, Tommy? In the bar? The Leeward Inn?"

Each answer was about fifteen seconds late. "No. . . . You don't want me. . . . I am sorry."

I sat on the unmade bed below the window. He offered the comics page. I said no thank you and he put the paper on the nightstand. For a minute we watched the lengthening afternoon shadows.

"Who are you, then?" I whispered. "What's your name?"

He leaned back in the wheelchair. The fist still rested in his lap. "Was a time," he began. "Years ago. I was a young man. . . ."

"Go on, please. . . ."

He was looking out the window with that same strange smile. "My wife. We got a car. A 'forty-seven Buick sedan. We drive it on Sundays. Today is Sunday." He pointed to the comics page as proof. "Go out in the country. Watch the colors change. Watch the leaves." Silence again.

"What's your name? What's your wife's name?"

"We stop at a garden restaurant. It's Swiss, they got polka Sunday afternoons. Red checked tablecloths. You married?"

I shook my head.

"I order beer, she drinks lemonade. She is so beautiful. A pretty flower dress and a sweater over her shoulders. First time I saw her she smiled at me."

136

I racked my brain for the name of Tommy's wife. It was in the documents at the Hall of Records. Lorna, Loretta . . .

"Leona," I said. "Her name was Leona."

The wrinkled face showed no reaction. "So soft, that sweater. She was younger than me. I'm old."

He nodded to himself, focusing on something in the distance. At first I was certain that this was Tommy Malakis. Now I didn't know at all. Max was small and frail, smaller than Michael's description. If he was Malakis, he was either a true amnesiac—in which case he couldn't have written that note—or a very shrewd man.

Last chance. I handed him Eddie's photograph of the dirty old city bus by the creek, with Cremmins in the foreground and Geraghty a fuzzy image in the back, circled in pen. I pointed to the circle.

"Do you know him?"

Max took the photo in a shaky hand and held it up to the light. I watched for the slightest reaction. *I wish I could see his eyes*, I thought. He turned over the photo a couple of times. Finally he handed it back.

"That ain't her," he said.

"No, no, that's not what I meant. . . ." Give it up. I pocketed the photo. If he knew Reuben Murtaugh, the bum in his doorway, he would have known Geraghty, who was Murtaugh's shadow. If he was Malakis, that is. Only Michael would know for sure.

Max waited patiently, expecting me to produce another photograph, this time of the woman he had loved many years ago. *Damn it, Tommy*, I wanted to burst out. *They're digging up your treasure. What are you going to do about it?*

But I kept quiet. This could be any sad old man, about to be discharged into the real world, memories hopelessly jumbled in his weakening mind. Leave him alone.

Max was looking at me for the first time, his wizened face warm with paternal affection. He raised his unclenched hand, like a benediction from the Pope.

"Goodbye," he said. He wasn't addressing anyone in particular. The fist in his lap remained closed. "I am sorry." That was directed at me.

As expected, Dr. Barrett was standing in the hallway. He had changed into a polo shirt and slacks. "Well?"

"It's not him," I said.

"I'm sorry."

"That's what he said." I wished that I had told a story that would have kept the issue open. "Why the wheelchair?"

"Claims his legs hurt. We can't find anything physically wrong with him. Sometimes he walks around with a cane. Most of the time not."

We had reached the outer door when the sound broke out, shattering the peace: a piteous wail. At first I thought it was a siren. But it wasn't mechanical. More like a wounded animal.

It continued for about ten seconds. Dr. Barrett looked apologetic. "He does that sometimes," he said. "Out of nowhere. No set time or reason. Been a while since the last one."

He was holding the door. I felt like an intruder. I wanted to hear that inhuman sound again, at the same time dreading it. There had been anguish in it, and deep sadness. Most of all, pain: endless, and intense, and terribly private.

19

Sitting before the fire, sipping a cognac, trees rustling in the wind outside. Sara Ludlow's living room was a sanctuary. An entire wall was lined with books; a thick rug covered the hardwood floor, and heavy beams crossed the ceiling. The house was at least sixty years old, complete with front porch swing and giant elms flanking the entrance.

On the other side of the fireplace sat Sara, a professorial woman of fifty, immersed in a casebook. It was Sunday night, beginning of a new week, and only three days from the developers' public meeting. I knew I had to return to San Francisco, if only to tie up loose ends, but I didn't want to. Here I was safe from Louis Boudeaux. Unfortunately, he was safe from me, and as long as I had no hard evidence to link him with Sherman's murder, he would remain so.

"Damn!" I muttered as two dozen felt pens slipped off my lap onto the floor. I had Sherman's notebook and twenty sheets of my own gibberish, feeble attempts to crack his paranoiac code. I got to my knees and began gathering them up for another try.

Sara looked up from her book. "Why don't you show it to a cryptographer? I know a professor at Berkeley who might be able to help."

"Why don't I just forget it? Maybe I ought to just hand the

whole thing over to Boudeaux and let *him* try to make something of the mess. Come to think of it, if he saw this book, he'd probably leave me alone. Whatever his scam is, it's a secret forever."

A secret important enough to kill for. I retrieved the last felt pen—peacock green—drained the snifter of cognac, and went back to the code.

A few minutes later I was staring into the fire again. It would be so easy to wrap up the whole affair right now. Let Boudeaux have his notebook, the charts, even the felt pens if he wanted them. Go to the cops with what I knew about the Tuttle murder, and let them make the case. Forget about the little man living in a clinic hidden by apple orchards. Let Malakis rest in peace, alive or dead. Bingo: two cases laid to rest, just like that.

"You know, there's absolutely no reason why you can't start on our cases while you're still living in San Francisco," Sara was saying. "Take some files back with you, do the research at one of the law libraries. That way when you're ready to move, you'll already be in the swing of things."

"Sure," I said vaguely. "If you don't mind working it like that."

"If nothing else, it would keep you occupied. If I were you, I would be going crazy from inactivity right now."

I had told Sara about Sherman's death and that Boudeaux was a suspect, but nothing more. As for the Malakis case, she knew only that Michael was battling Sunrise Development and looking for a missing person. As far as she was concerned I was hanging out at the Nick of America, nursing my broken body, bored out of my skull. Well, I thought, be grateful for small things. At least I'm not bored.

Sara was standing over me, pouring another cognac. Her piercing gaze could reach right into my thoughts, and she was giving me one now.

"Sara—" I started. I wanted so much to confide in this caring woman, to tell her about Tommy Malakis, about the man in the clinic and his sad memories of a nameless woman in a print dress. Sara would know what to do. She always hit on the right course of action, the one I never seemed able to discover for myself. But I had confided in too many people already. Tommy, Max, Michael, Harry, Emma Whaley—I had placed them all in jeopardy, and their safety was my responsibility.

"Out with it," said Sara. "What's on your mind?"

I took the snifter from her and managed to raise a smile intended to exude confidence. "Nothing," I said.

Three hours later, Sara had gone to bed, the fire was reduced to embers, and I was still bent over the notebook. Pages and pages of failed attempts at decoding it were spread over the floor, mixed with felt markers and colored pencils. For the thousandth time I stared at the groups of colored letters: IAEED, .CMNO, SSSLS, ERLRD, etc. Seven colors, and a group of numbers—39.3.1—at the top of the page. It looked like a date: March 1, 1939, or January 3, 1939. It also added up to sixteen. Regroup the numbers slightly, and it was 13-39. Thirteen times three is thirty-nine. An unlucky number tripled. So what?

What else could it be? Again I tried to correlate it to the volume number or pages of a book. But what book? One that only Sherman owned? Not likely; if he were to lose his only copy of a rare volume, then the code would become a mystery to him, too.

He had given me a key for safekeeping. I was intended to be privy to the mysteries. *You are the only person I can trust.* Foreseeing his own death, he had handed the torch of knowledge and paranoia to me.

I thought back over what words I could remember, cursing myself for not having taken notes. A real investigator would have. *They are conducting experiments.* Science books, catalogues—too vague. Something about a *web of circumstance,* about connections between things. He had mentioned that twice. A *coup? I suspect a coup.* Kings, governments, politics. That was promising, but it didn't refer to anything specific, unless he thought Michael was planning to take over the city. *I will be a witness against the sorcerers.* Magicians, experiments again. A lot of baby talk. *Remember the prophets.* No, *Remember the words of the prophets*. I leapt up and started scanning Sara's wall of books.

The Bible on the top shelf, upper left. Balancing on a chair, I pulled it down and opened it. The last time was one year ago, when Father Tedesco read to me from the Book of Job. *For the arrows of the Almighty are within me, the poison whereof drinketh up my spirit: the terrors of God do set themselves in array against me.*

But it was the prophets with whom Sherman apparently was concerned, and I leafed through them. Isaiah, Jeremiah, Ezekiel, Daniel, Lamentations . . . which one?

The numbers held the key. 39.3.1. If 39 was the thirty-ninth book of the Old Testament—Sherman didn't strike me as the New Testament sort—then he was referring to Malachi, the last book. I turned to chapter 3, verse 1.

Twenty minutes later I knew where Tommy Malakis was hiding, and who Sherman Tuttle was—and two cases became one.

20

---

*Behold, I will send my messenger, and he shall pre-
pare the way before me: and the Lord, whom ye seek, shall
suddenly come to his temple, even the messenger of the covenant, whom ye delight in: behold, he shall come, saith the
Lord of hosts.*

Malachi 3:5 was familiar, too: *And I will come near to you
to judgment; and I will be a swift witness against the sorcerers. . . .* No need to decode Tuttle's notebook to know
who he was. But I couldn't sleep now.

I printed the entire verse of Malachi 3:1, and under it the
alphabet, so *Behold* became ABCDEF, and so on. When the
alphabet ran out, I started it again. When I was finished, I
had printed it seven times, with ABC left over at the end to
even things up. Now the colors. Think like Sherman. His
was an orderly insanity, so I put the seven colors in order of
the spectrum: red, orange, yellow, green, blue, purple, and
black at the end. I colored the seven alphabets in that order,
dropping the three leftover letters.

I turned to the cipher. The first five letters were IAEED:
orange, purple, green, purple, and green. I looked in the
key for the first orange I of the quotation, in order to match
it to the letter below, followed by the next purple A, and so
on.

It didn't work. There was no orange I at all, and even ignoring that stumbling block I came up with (?)CIAG. Sherman's secret apparently was more random than I had thought.

But not necessarily. If instead of coloring each *alphabet* a different color I changed colors with every *letter*, still in the order of the spectrum, I had a completely different key. Now the ABCDEF that corresponded to *Behold* was red, orange, yellow, green, blue, and purple. And Sherman's language began to unravel.

You kept running through the quotation, finding the next designated colored letter, starting over when you got to the end. A few letters came out wrong, until I realized that periods weren't meant to end sentences, but signified that you were to skip a letter: D., colored green, meant go to the *second* green D in the key. A single sentence easily ran through all seven alphabets, meaning that a yellow O, for example, could stand for more than one letter, depending on which alphabet it was taken from. And because Sherman kept changing his quotations—each one was keyed to numbers at the beginning of the blocks of letters—it was impossible to decode the message by counting the number of times a single colored letter appeared. You had to have the Bible in front of you.

What I was looking for appeared on the very first page of the notebook. The decoded message was all too familiar, right down to the misspelling: I AM COMING BACK. TELL NO ONE. I WILL BE COMING BACK FOR MY TRESHURE. HELP ME. Malakis, Malachi. The messenger of the covenant. Had I known the Bible better, I would have figured it out right away. Sherman Tuttle was Malakis's messenger. Malakis used Tuttle to communicate with Michael, the only man he trusted to help find his "treasure." That was what brought Tuttle to The Wayside in the first place. But were Malakis and Max the same person?

The proof could be anywhere in the notebook. I would be laboring over the cipher until sunrise. And who could say that the effort would pay off? Sherman Tuttle probably had a dozen secret codes and languages to mask his obsessions.

Languages . . . something was nagging at me, blocked by a brain deprived of sleep. Secret languages. Like the one invented by the people of Boonville. What was it called? Boontling.

I had thrown away the Boonville newspaper, souvenir of the Anderson Valley Clinic. I fished it out of Sara's trash and found the article. Boontling had words for nearly everything. Even baseball. The word for baseball was *buzzchick*. For home run, *rude eye*. What Sherman Tuttle had said the day of the softball game between the restaurants. Not baby talk, not nonsense. The language of an Anderson Valley native, or at least someone who had appropriated it for his own use.

I had never asked whether Tuttle was a former patient at the Anderson Valley Clinic. I dialed the clinic now.

It was three in the morning. A woman answered. I asked for Dr. Barrett, trying to put some urgency into my voice.

"I'm sorry, he's not at the clinic tonight. This is the night nurse. May I help you?"

Whoever she was, she was my only hope. "Please pass this message along to Dr. Barrett and the rest of your staff. You have a patient there called Max. He's an amnesiac. Do you know who I am talking about?"

"Yes, but—"

"Dr. Barrett said the clinic is about to release him. Don't do it. Stall him, hold up the paperwork, just for a few hours until I can get there. And don't let anybody see him. Do you understand? I'm a relative; the name is Thorpe. Max's life may be in danger."

"Would you hold the line, please?"

I plotted the events of the next few hours. It would take about an hour to get to the clinic. I could make it before sunrise. Then I would bring Malakis back to Sara's, where he would be safe. Then to San Francisco—

The nurse came back on the line. "Miss Thorpe?"

"Yes."

"You say you're a relative?"

"Yes, I'm his . . . niece, but it's more important than that. This is a police matter."

"I'm sorry, but Max checked out early this evening."

Of course he did. The dread that had been lurking deep inside me welled up with full force. I was too late, had known that I would be.

I asked who took him away.

"There's no other name here. He's the one who signed the papers."

Dr. Barrett wouldn't have minded. After all, he needed the bed. But that was purest cynicism. I knew it was really my fault. In effect, I had told Barrett that Max wasn't my problem. I was afraid to admit that he was Malakis. That would have meant taking responsibility for him, protecting him from the jackals.

"If you'd like to speak to Dr. Barrett, he'll be back on Tuesday—"

I hung up. How long would it take a man in Malakis's condition to get to San Francisco? He could have made it on a Greyhound by now; he already had a ticket. I grabbed my coat and Sherman's diary and calculated how fast *I* could get back to the city. Fast enough to save a life, I prayed.

The eastern sky was reddening over Mount Diablo as I approached the Golden Gate Bridge. Warm air was rising off the Bay, and there wasn't a wisp of fog. Indian summer at last—for San Francisco, the finest weather of the year.

Tommy had more presence of mind than I thought. He had managed to conceal his sanity from everyone. Of course, no one had any reason to dig for the truth. He was safe in his hiding place until I came along.

I was certain he was going back to San Francisco. Landfall would either be The Wayside or the site of his old bar. Logic would conclude that he'd make straight for Michael Sloane, but he might be running scared from him as well—because I had mentioned Michael by name. He was in danger and he knew it. I remembered showing Tommy the photograph of Cremmins and Geraghty. I was batting a thousand on this one.

Then there was Cremmins. Dr. Barrett said that Tommy had stepped in front of the bus "for no apparent reason." It was probably just chance that the two crossed paths in

Ukiah. Seeing Tommy alive, Cremmins's pickled brain remembered the treasure story, and Ukiah's town bum took decisive action for the first time in his life. Maybe the idiot even thought it was finally safe to return to San Francisco.

I pulled up to my office—parking is never a problem at five in the morning—to make some phone calls. It was a good base of operations from which to start.

At first I didn't notice the beat-up American car parked up ahead. I was thinking of other things as I stepped into the street. Even when the doors swung open, I paid no attention. It was when the two men climbed out that I suspected. Then they came toward me and there was no question at all. I jumped back in the car, jammed the lock, and tried to start the engine at the same time. No such luck. The damned thing wouldn't turn over. No second chance. A window shattered. Now I couldn't get my door unlocked. They helped me. Dragged me out, slapped a knife to my throat. "Shut up, just shut up," one of them hissed, twisting my sore arm and shoving me forward. Just like the guy in the holding cell. Louis Boudeaux's trademark. I was thrown into their car and off we went.

21

I forgot to mention the blindfold, but really I don't remember when it was put on. There was just this sudden awareness that I was in darkness, in a car that was moving very fast. I was wedged into the floor of the back seat, and somebody's foot was jamming me down. Pain stampeded through my body, unfocused, unrelenting. Taking corners was torture; the driver seemed to be whipping around them on purpose. Here we were, one block from the Hall of Justice and the single biggest concentration of cops in the city of San Francisco, and I was being kidnapped in a car going at least twice the speed limit, and nobody saw it. For some reason it helped to know this. It brought on an indignation, even anger, that masked my fear. No longer was I thinking only of what they would do to me. Now it was: I'll get you, you bastards.

The car lurched to a stop. I was dragged out and led up some steep stairs. We went through a door and I was shoved down on what felt like a couch. I reached for the soaking blindfold, but somebody gently took my hand away.

I sat there shivering for a long time, listening to sounds. Walking, rustling, coughing. Cars going by outside. People murmuring from across the room. Their voices were calm and measured. As if they were waiting for a golf tournament to begin.

I heard the rustling of paper, or maybe a paper bag, and somebody approached. I felt the warmth of his breath. He was crouched before me. My body tensed up against my will. Here it comes. A gun, a knife, a baseball bat. It was worse not knowing what to expect in this strangely silent room. I only wished I could control the shivers.

"Take my hand," said a soft voice.

What? The words didn't register.

"Take my hand," he repeated in the same tone. And waited.

I wanted to obey, didn't want to make anybody mad. Yet I imagined putting my hand into a meat grinder. How badly would that hurt? My hand rose to hold his. It was cold and slack. Still a tingle shot up my arm.

"Three days ago I sent you a message. Do you know what I'm talking about?" The voice was calm, almost friendly. "Do you know who I am?"

I nodded.

"Yes. At that time you were told to surrender a piece of my property that you happen to be hiding from me. Now I will ask you again. Will you hand it over and be done with it?"

I skipped the usual I-don't-know-what-you're-talking-about bit. I wasn't angry anymore, just terrified. The last thing I wanted to do was piss this nice man off.

But I couldn't speak. My mouth and throat were dead dry.

I took my hand away. "Give it back," he commanded. There was tension in his voice now.

I gripped his hand. The voice was calm again. "Now sister, I want you to think real, real carefully about what is on the line here. I have a very large investment to protect, but I make no unnecessary trouble. That is a fine way to get busted, understand? So I'm going to be fair, give you a real chance to make good. Take another twenty-four hours to come up with the stuff. Everything you got of Sherman Tuttle's. Hand it over and that's the end of your worries. Fair enough?"

He wanted an answer now. I had to say something. He seemed so reasonable. Now's my chance to end this nonsense and survive. If only I could speak . . . but I was in a kind of spell, a bizarre mixture of terror and comfort. He knew exactly what he was doing. This man had murdered and mutilated a helpless bum, and God knows how many others, yet I desperately wanted him to *like* me. And that made me ill.

"I don't have it," I said.

A deadly silence, as I waited for the agony, wondered how long it would last.

"Take my hand," was all he said, ever friendly.

I shook my head in bewilderment, still holding his hand. "Take my hand." Was he mad?

The others in the room started to snicker. What was I missing?

"Shake," he said.

Completely lost, eager to participate in the joke, I pumped his hand. It dropped into my lap.

Instinctively I touched it, felt the cold joints of the fingers, the rough hairs, and the wrist that terminated in a stump.

I shot to my feet, and maybe I screamed, knocking the foul thing away, instantly getting the "joke." Sherman Tuttle's missing hand. What we'll do to *you*. Two people grabbed me by the arms. I was going to throw up. A towel was shoved in my face to keep it off the carpet.

A paging beeper went off. The nice man was speaking again. "Have it in your office by nine A.M. tomorrow," he said as I was led away. I sensed the door opening. Then I was hit by a blast of fresh air.

They dropped me off a block from the office. I saw the car again as it sped away—a dark blue, American-model sedan—but that was all I saw. It was maddening to be harassed repeatedly by faceless enemies—in the alley, in the holding cell, and now on a public street. It blurred my sense of resolve. I had to keep reminding myself what was important: find Tommy Malakis.

Returning to my car, I surveyed the smashed window. Glass was all over the seat. I was surprised to find my purse still there. It had fallen to the floor in the scuffle, out of sight. A car with a smashed window in that neighborhood was assumed to have been picked clean. As for the code-book, it was in my overnight bag in the trunk. Boudeaux's henchmen hadn't even bothered to search the car. I retrieved the purse and headed for my office.

I was about to undertake the major project of climbing the stairs when I heard voices. "Get yo' ass away from me!" somebody yelled. "Hold him down!" another man barked. A garbage can overturned with a bang that echoed down the alley. I headed in the direction of the fracas. The first voice had been Elroy's.

Sure enough, Elroy was pinned to the ground by two cops, one of whom was Officer Martin Kessler. He had his nightstick out and was administering a series of blows to the helpless wino. "Aaaaagh!" Elroy yelled. "Motherfucker!" Then he let loose with the foulest string of epithets I had ever heard, even South of Market. At times like this Elroy could drop his cute act.

"Leave him alone!" I cried out, loping toward the cops as fast as I could, given the state of my wrecked body. Kessler continued to beat Elroy while the other one held him down. I was running now, despite my injuries, and I was boiling over. The rage that had been building in me over the last hour—no, the last two and a half weeks—exploded. My eyes were burning, my limbs shaking. I grabbed Kessler's arm and tried to jerk the weapon away. He turned in astonishment. "What the fuck—" he said. His partner released Elroy and pounced at me. My good arm flailed out and caught him just below the throat. Then I bent low and jammed an elbow in Kessler's balls. He screamed and crumpled to the ground. His partner grabbed me, swung me around, and pinned my arms back. I didn't feel a thing. Tried to kick his shins but he had a leg wrapped around my ankles. I kicked again, hit my purse, and it went skittering across the sidewalk, spilling its contents. My gun flew out and lay on the ground like an exclamation point.

Kessler was back on his feet and about to grab me when Elroy jumped him from behind. It was a feeble effort. "Go get 'em, sweetie!" the wino cried, riding the bewildered cop. He shook off Elroy easily and helped his partner to shove me against the police car. I was still hyperventilating. Through the pounding in my ears I heard the handcuffs ratchet and click into place. "Son of a bitch, Marty," the cop cried. "Now it's the ladies, too! This street is getting *mean!*"

22

"And then I says to him, 'You bastard. Didn't nobody ever teach you how to treat a lady? You think you can just come in here and beat the shit outta me whenever the moon is full? I don't gotta take it! Know what your problem is? You don't respect women! That's right, you dick!' And he's just standin' there, you know, starin' at the floor, holdin' the goddamn fry pan, just like a little boy! Well, I told *him*. Fifth time he's beat me up in the last month. Problem is, I don't think he loves me no more."

The heavyset woman with stringy hair took a drag on her cigarette butt and flicked it away. She was holding court at the far end of the locked holding area at the Hall of Justice, surrounded by four other women. The rest were slumped against the wall, smoking or talking in low tones. I occupied a bench in the corner, next to a bank of vending machines. Torn and dirty clothes, unbrushed hair, purple and yellow skin: I looked just like the rest of them.

The bench was rock hard and there was barely room to sit upright, but I was drifting in and out of sleep anyway, head sinking to my chest and snapping awake every few minutes. I hadn't slept in more than twenty-four hours, since Saturday night, and even that wasn't much of a rest. I was hungry, too, having been thrown in jail right after breakfast. And I craved a shower.

The adrenaline rush had long since subsided, leaving me nauseous and aching all over. The anger was still there, though, in the form of a simmering resolve awaiting release. Right now I wasn't going anywhere. I could guess the charges: assaulting an officer, interfering with an arrest, illegal possession of a firearm, disturbing the peace. And, of course, practicing investigation without a license. I was sure they would think of a few more. I didn't have a lot of friends on the police force.

My body was exhausted, but my mind was a jumble of thoughts, like a race car spinning its wheels in sludge. Got to get out of here. Sonia will be here soon to bail me out. Art Shade will be happy to put up the money; he likes me. Worry about the charges later.

Half asleep, I felt shrouded in thick, warm wool. Against my will it came back, the dream in the church with the stained-glass windows bleeding light. Usually I managed to fight it off during waking hours, but my exhaustion had rendered me helpless. So I was kneeling again at the altar, for the hundredth time. But it wasn't a dream; it was a waking nightmare. *It happened,* I thought, and a chill shot through me. One year ago, almost to the day.

People used to ask me, when I was a public defender, "How can you defend such scum? What do you do when you know they're guilty?" At every meeting with strangers, at every dinner party, I would come up against it. "Say that you *know* a guy is guilty, and you spring him on some technicality, and he goes off and commits another crime. How can you live with yourself?" But people don't understand. They think that's the worst thing that can happen.

Being a public defender is playing a game, of course: just like being a judge, or a district attorney. But good P.D.s *believe* in what they're doing, if not in the innocence of their clients. Maybe he *is* scum, you say, but he'll get a fair break from me. The best of public defenders can stand up in court and defend the worst of criminals. That's the way it's supposed to work.

But every once in a while the rules of the game change. All of a sudden you've got a client who is *innocent*; you know it in your heart. And you throw yourself into the trial. Now the moral anguish weighs on the shoulders of the district attorney, and you're the champion of justice. All those years of rationalizing, distinguishing among endless shades of gray—for this moment of purest black and white. You click in.

In my nine years as a public defender I was blessed with half a dozen such cases. Leonard Wheelock was one—a quiet, intelligent boy of seventeen, who worked in a gas station until the night a thirteen-year-old girl was raped and stabbed sixteen times just two blocks away. She lived, but she hasn't spoken a word since. Wheelock was arrested for the crime. The evidence was a bloody rag found in the parking lot of the gas station; the testimony of a janitor who was in a building across the street when he saw someone running away, wearing a mechanic's uniform; and the fact that no one had bought gas at the time of the crime, so the accused had no alibi. All that, plus the fact that Wheelock was black, which in itself is enough to convict a man in San Francisco.

It was my finest moment. Time after time I countered the prosecution's subtlest ploys; my character witnesses were flawless, and every objection I made was dead on target. I never gave a better closing argument. The courtroom was silent for at least a minute after I sat down in triumph. When it was over the jury came back with a verdict of not guilty in exactly fourteen minutes: a new record for the public defender's office.

That night we celebrated, Sonia and some other P.D.s and I, and while we were out, Leonard Wheelock came looking for me at my father's restaurant. I had no idea that he knew of the place. It was closing time, and Joseph, Bernard, and my mother had gone home. Only my father was there, cleaning up. When Wheelock didn't find me, he killed Nick Mastrangelo, my father, a kind old man who had urged me to become a public defender because he identified with "the underdogs." Stabbed him more than a dozen times.

At four o'clock that morning I was taken to the police station to identify the murderer. We sat across from each other, a sliver of wire mesh between us, and he looked at me through the dull film of his eyes, with a nasty little smirk. There was blood on his clothes. Someone said he had already made a statement. Said he went to the restaurant to find *me*, not my father, to rape me like he did that little girl. Then came the words, all he said to me, his explanation of what had happened. Words that shrieked through my ears, that still do on bad nights, even though they were delivered so quietly and naturally that their meaning didn't sink in at first:

"I wanted to thank you for what you did."

Two days later I knelt in the church at my father's funeral mass, and the grief and the guilt poured forth as everyone stood by and watched, and my serenity was shattered forever.

The door of the holding area opened, and there stood Sonia, towering over the bailiff with the keys. "Let's get the heck out of here, girl," she said, taking me by the arm.

"Don't worry," Sonia was saying as we walked into the light of day. "These charges don't amount to a thing, and they know it. If they try to take you to trial, we will *stomp* them."

Through the glare I watched the derelicts go by outside the Hall of Justice. One was passed out on the strip of lawn; a Labrador retriever sniffed him and peed on a nearby bush. Another stood motionless across the street, arm raised high, middle finger pointing at the sky. He was flipping off the world. And a crazy man was pacing before the steps, shouting at the top of his lungs: "Yes, ladies, here we are! We're here at the Howl of Justice! That's right, what I said, the Hooooowl of Justice! Lawd have mercy one time!" Drunks, crazies, weenie-wagglers, apostates: they were the same unfortunates I saw every day, but they looked different. For the people living on the street, every day was a battle for survival, a search for sanctuary. They were no longer abstract pieces of "unfinished business." I was through running away. I would find Tommy Malakis.

Part Three

23

I must have looked like just another bum, banging on the doors of The Wayside, shouting out Michael Sloane's name. It was noon, and the morning meal had been served and cleared away. Last night's guests had been kicked out until the four P.M. bed sign-up.

Finally the door was unlocked. Michael's jaw dropped. I was getting used to the effect that my appearance had on people.

"Christ, Cass." He pulled me inside. "I heard you were in the bucket. Who did this to you? *Who*, damn it?"

"Oh, you name it—psychos, dope dealers, cops, dogs. They've all had a shot at me in the last few days."

"I should never have gotten you involved, that was incredibly stupid of me," said Michael, unable to take his eyes off my latest bruises. "We've got to get you to a doctor."

We entered the common sleeping room, or *slugging nook* in Boontling. It looked huge when empty. "There's no time," I said. "Tommy needs help."

"Will you forget about that? It ends right now, right here. I don't want you having anything more to do with Malakis. Next time you'll get your neck broken."

"I found him."

"First a doctor, then the police—*what*?"

"I said I found him. Then I lost him. I was hoping he would come here."

"No, he hasn't, at least I don't think so . . . but where? And what about *you*? I haven't seen you for five days, I called your house, I had just about given up. . . ."

"I didn't know you cared."

"Give me a break."

Michael paced the floor as I told him about the clinic, Sherman Tuttle, how I found the codebook, and Geraghty. It was a relief to unburden myself.

"That's just great," he moaned when I was done. "We almost had him, now he could be anywhere. Dead, for that matter."

"Well, I'm sorry, but I didn't know for sure until I decoded the notebook—"

"All right," Michael said, holding up a hand. "I'm not blaming anyone. We'll look everywhere, and we *will* find him. But first, a doctor for you."

"I don't need a doctor," I snapped. I was, however, having trouble standing. I settled myself onto a cot. "I need to get cleaned up. Had a little run-in with Louis Boudeaux this morning."

Michael stopped pacing. "Boudeaux? What do you know about him?"

"Oh, only that he wants to kill me. He's been inquiring about Tuttle's notebook. He seems to think there's something in it that will compromise him."

"This is great. Let me tell you what *I* know. I've been checking up on Tuttle, like you asked me to. And get this. Word has it he was hanging around the headquarters of Mr. Louis Boudeaux, one of our city's most successful businessmen. I understand Tuttle had to be rousted a couple of times."

"'Rousted' seems a little tame, considering what happened to him."

"You say he wants that notebook?"

"Another understatement."

"Then get it to the police. *Now.*"

"But I haven't finished decoding it."

"What the hell difference does it make? What is this, a cereal box contest? Give 'em the code, too—"

"Not yet. I've got things to do first."

Michael sat on the cot across from me. "Cass, listen to me. Are you listening?"

"Uh-huh."

"Over the weekend I tried to reach you. Called you at home, at the restaurant, called Sonia . . . I even looked for that worthless ex-husband of yours. Nobody seemed to know where you were."

"I told you—"

"Yeah, but I didn't know that then. The point is, after we talked last week, I got to thinking about what a shit-heel I've been—"

"You've already told me about what a shit-heel you've been. Many times."

"Will you *listen* to me, please? Christ, this is difficult. I'm trying to say I fucked up, getting you involved in this mess. You know me, I get hung up on these ideas of mine, and sometimes I forget about *people*. People I care about. Well, you can see where it got me. At least one innocent man has already been wiped out, and the biggest dope dealer in the fucking Western world is out for *your* ass . . . all because of me."

"I'm a free woman. I accepted the cases."

"After I just about broke your arm—sorry, bad choice of words. Anyway, all those things you said about me were true, and I'd like to make up for it, and I think you should drop all of this before you *die*."

"You express yourself so gracefully."

"Fuck grace. If I have to shock you into good sense, I will. Whatever it takes."

I lay on the cot, staring at the ceiling of the stark room. Michael was asking the impossible, and he probably knew it. I suppose he thought it was worth a try.

"Sorry," I said. "I have to see this through."

Michael moved over to my cot and sat beside me. "You are the stubbornest person I know. Next to myself, of course."

That was a fair evaluation. But for Michael, it was stubbornness with a purpose. Despite his flamboyant style, he really was accomplishing something at The Wayside—more than I could ever hope to do. While I was busy mapping my escape route, he was sticking it out on skid row. Michael never agonized over where he belonged.

He placed a cool hand on my forehead and brushed the strands of hair away from my eyes.

"I look like hell," I said.

"Impossible." He caressed my hair, then my face. First time in more than a year that someone had touched me that way. First time in weeks that I had felt anything but pain. Just to lie here for a while . . .

Michael leaned over and without hesitation gave me a prolonged kiss. I didn't turn away. Resolve was flowing out of my body; wonderful relaxation was taking over, and something else too.

I sat up, taking his hand for a moment. "I'll call you."

He sighed, but let me come to my feet.

"You'll let me know if Malakis shows up?" I asked.

"I'll let you know. Please be careful."

"I'm always careful," I said as I limped to the door.

When I stepped out of The Wayside, Phillip Harrington, Jr., was waiting.

"I understand you were arrested."

"Leave me alone."

I started down the street, Harrington tagging along. "Any comment on your arrest?"

"Why don't you go stick your head in an oven?"

"That kind of talk isn't very constructive. You found him, didn't you?"

"Found who?"

"Malakis. Where is he hiding? If you trust me, I promise to keep it confidential. The story will break exactly when you want it to. Provided it's an exclusive, of course."

"Stop following me around."

"Who's following? I see you here and there. And I can deduce things. I know you're on the case unofficially now, and that's fine with me. My status on this story is a bit unofficial too, so it's not as if I had to answer to an editor. My point is, I don't have to file copy by the six o'clock deadline. If you trust me, I'll wait for the story to happen. I have never broken a promise to a source."

A shriveled derelict with a nose the size and shape of a potato stepped in front of Harrington. "Listen, man, listen—"

"I don't have the time—" Harrington started.

"No, man, listen listen listen," the beggar said. "Just listen for one second. You see, I got to get across the Bay on BART, man, and I only got twenty-one cents, I just need a dollar to get home to a hot meal and a happy wife—"

I stepped around the man and kept going, leaving Harrington behind. "Hey, wait!" he called out, shoving the beggar aside and catching up. "I was sincere about what I said. I only broke the story last time out of sheer ignorance."

"You got that right."

"I had no *idea* it was supposed to be a secret. Thought you'd appreciate the publicity. Now I know better. Let's work something out. Let's collaborate."

Everybody wants to collaborate. We reached my car. "Mr. Harrington," I said. "Eat it."

"Now is that kind of rudeness appropriate? I merely asked you politely—"

The potato-nosed man was tugging on Harrington's corduroy jacket. "Hey! My man, my man, my *man!*"

Harrington tried to brush him away like a piece of lint. "Get away from me, will you?"

The hand returned, pulling at Harrington's lapels. "Hey, Fritzy! Come over here! This the guy we met coupla weeks ago at Sally Ann! You remember, don'tcha?"

Three other street types sauntered over, regarding Harrington like some form of laboratory animal. "Sally Ann" is slang for the Salvation Army.

"Man, do you look *different,*" the first one said as the others fingered the leather piping of the reporter's frayed jacket. Harrington tried unsuccessfully to shrug them off.

163

"You was filthy as a mud puddle back then. You have really fixed yourself up!"

"He's a inspiration," somebody else said.

"Hey, help us out, brother!" one of them wailed as Harrington tried to push him away. I slipped into my car and drove off. In the rearview mirror I saw Harrington free himself and dive into the car that had been parked behind mine. I turned a couple of corners and lost him.

24

The mercury was up to ninety by the time I pulled up to my house. Malakis wouldn't come out of hiding until nightfall. Until then I would be busy every moment. I prayed that Boudeaux would keep his promise and leave me alone until tomorrow morning.

Something was wrong. I knew it before I put the key in the door. The knob was loose, and there were scratches around the latch. The shades were pulled in every window. I opened the door and slipped into the hallway.

Inside it was airless and still, heat trapped by the sealed windows.

I crept to the living room, hugging the wall. Peered into the dimness. Empty. Nothing disturbed. No one hiding behind a couch, ready to pounce. No one I could see.

On down the hallway toward the bedrooms. The spare one, where Eddie was supposed to be sleeping, was unoccupied. No sheets on the bed, no suitcase on the floor. Eddie was neat, but not that neat. I moved along, stood now in the doorway of my bedroom.

The blanket was thrown aside, the sheets crumpled. A man's sock protruded from beneath the bed. The bastard. I told him to sleep in the other room.

Bathroom next. Always hated bathrooms in scenes like

this one, too many movies where the heroine rips aside the shower curtain to reveal . . . nothing. What the hell am I doing? Creeping around my own house. No apologies. Plenty of reason to be paranoid. No, not paranoid. Justifiably terrified. Better check the kitchen.

So back down the hall, another glimpse into the bedrooms, and into an empty, undisturbed kitchen. Only the garage left. The button lock was sticking out. Supposed to be locked. I pushed open the door and looked upon . . .

Devastation.

I heard myself gasp. Even in the dim light of the garage I could see them right away, the jukeboxes pushed out of place, smashed, toppled over. Someone had taken a hammer to the Seeburg, reducing the works to splinters of glass and plastic and dust. A '59 Wurlitzer lay on its side, disemboweled. The Rock-Ola looked as if it had been in a head-on collision at fifty miles an hour. Shards of colored glass crunched underfoot, and the floor was covered with pieces of records.

The meanness of it all was incomprehensible, hatred directed at these beautiful machines. Pure malevolence. Then I began to wonder about Eddie. I pictured him smashed to bits, too, flesh and blood mixed up in the circuitry. A shiver of despair ran through me as I stepped into the garage. The door shut with a slam. A shadow flew at me—no, a man, swinging a tire iron and yelling like a savage. He took a chunk out of the wall above my head. I collapsed to the floor in a rain of plaster. The man towered over me, chest heaving. It was Joseph.

"Jesus!" He dropped the tire iron and slumped into the debris beside me. "Man, I thought they'd come back. I was gonna take 'em out this time."

I took a few days to catch my breath. "Oh my God," I finally managed. Then, "Where's Eddie?"

"What was that lop doin' here, anyway?" Joseph demanded. "I come over to check on you, and he's gettin' his ass kicked to hell and back by a coupla black dudes. I mean they're smashin' up your house, and I'm thinkin' they've killed you or somethin', so I go after 'em . . . well, I guess I saved the life of that piece of shit, and I can't say I'm glad. How the hell'd he get in here?"

"I let him stay."

"That slime, how could—"

"Can it, Joseph, please, just *can* it!" A little too hysterical, but my nerves were still jangling. "I'm not in the mood for this right now."

Joseph helped me to my feet. "Sorry. But nobody told *me* what the hell was goin' on. I didn't know where you were, whether you was safe or what, and here's this guy gettin' his head knocked apart! I tell you, it don't make no sense to me."

It made plenty of sense to me. Boudeaux's men came looking for me last night. Instead they found Eddie.

Joseph followed me into the living room, where I fell into a chair, overcome by exhaustion. "Where's Eddie now?"

"He's in the hospital, that's where he is, and those two jerks ran off, even though I managed to smash 'em up pretty good, and if you think I'm gonna let you outta my sight from now on you're as crazy as everybody else is!"

I couldn't help smiling. Here was one of the few people in the world right now who didn't want to manipulate me, beat me up, steal something from me, or kill me. A comforting thought, even if Joseph could do nothing to help. I was truly on my own for the next few hours.

"Joseph, I need a favor," I said, stifling a yawn.

"You ask me anything. Just ask."

"Watch over my mother."

"Anything but—"

"She's all alone at the restaurant. I want someone with her. Now would you do this for me please?"

"In other words, 'Leave me alone,' right?"

"In other words, take care of her. I can take care of myself. The guys who did this won't be back for a while. And I promise I'll be safer if you stay away."

"Know what you oughta do? Take your mom's advice and get the hell outta town. That's the only way you'll really be safe, and you know it."

Santa Rosa seemed far away. Dragging my body out of the

chair, I kissed Joseph on the cheek. "You're all right," I said. He shook his head and left me alone.

Through the living room curtains I saw Phillip Harrington, Jr., waiting in his car across the street.

I let him wait while I grabbed a shower. It helped, although it took superhuman willpower not to collapse on the bed afterward and sleep for a couple of weeks. No time to sleep, I kept telling myself, until the repetitions started making me sleepy.

Harrington followed me out to San Francisco General, making no effort to conceal himself. In the parking lot he shouted as I stepped out of my car. "I know who you're going to see!" he said. "I've already been!"

A nurse gave me the room number, and I took the elevator to the fifth floor. The ward had six beds to a room, all occupied. A couple of patients were parked in wheelchairs out in the hallway.

My ex-husband's bed was by the window. Propped up on three pillows, he was reading *Sports Illustrated* and watching somebody on TV win a complete set of lawn furniture. He had two black eyes, a taped-up nose, a bandage covering the side of his face, and a cast on his left wrist.

"You look worse than me now," I said.

"Yo, Cass! All right! So you heard about those guys coming after me. Let me just say, they were total scum. Turning on me like that . . ."

"How badly are you hurt?"

"Aw, not too bad. I was holding my own. Your boyfriend showed up and we took 'em on together. I'm here 'cause I got insurance. Figured I'd take advantage of it."

"What about the film?"

"Oh, yeah, that. . . . I haven't got it anymore."

"They stole it? Did you make copies?"

Eddie perused the magazine with sudden interest. "Actually, it's not like that . . . we made a deal. I sold it to 'em."

"You *what*? After all that?"

"Okay, so run me down! It was a business deal. I knew what I was doing. Driving up the price, that's all."

"So much for your scathing documentary on insurance scams."

"That's still in development. You think I'd be scared away by a couple of punks like that?"

"Uh-huh."

"Well, go ahead and think that, I don't care. You'd seen these guys you might feel differently. My only mistake was in trusting the snakes in the first place. Three days ago I sell those photos to 'em, then last night they like turn around and do this for no apparent reason at all! Of course, they sent some different guys to rough me up, coupla black dudes in leather. But I know where they were from. And are we going to have a *lawsuit* . . . hey, maybe you'd like to represent me."

I stopped myself from telling Eddie who his attackers really were. Let him think that he was the target. Right now I needed Eddie in my debt, not the other way around.

"So. I let you stay in my house for a couple of nights, and your friends wreck the hell out of it. Thank you very much."

"You think I invited 'em? That shit with the jukeboxes really pissed me off! Imagine that." He shook his head, amazed at the lowlifes of the world.

"Tell you what. You can make it up to me." I threw a pair of jeans and a shirt on the bed. "Put these on, you're checking out."

"Huh? But I'm injured here. Doctors say I've gotta rest, and the insurance pays for three whole days—"

"Put them on and get *out!*" That tone always worked.

Eddie sighed and climbed out of bed, exaggerating his injuries with laborious movements. *I married this man,* I thought to myself for the thousandth time.

"Shit, that hurts!" he moaned, struggling into his pants. "Why are you doing this to me?"

"It's for my own good." I helped him on with the shirt, hurting myself more than him. "Come on," I urged, pulling him off the bed. He yelled again in mock pain.

We got past the nurses and the front desk without being questioned. At the entrance I surveyed the parking lot through the glass doors. Harrington was still waiting in his car, about fifty feet away. "Will you tell me what's going on here?" Eddie demanded.

"There's fifty bucks in the back pocket of your jeans," I said. "Here's my car keys. I want you to drive over the Bay Bridge and go north on Highway 80. Don't stop for anything; there's plenty of gas. Up around Richmond there's a Travelodge. You're already registered there. Check in, lock your door, don't answer the phone, watch TV, and spend the night in your room. Then tomorrow you can come back. Got it?"

"What am I supposed to do for food?" Harrington was watching as we walked to my car.

"Order room service."

"Travelodges haven't *got* room service! They don't even have ice machines!"

"Stop it, Eddie, you're exaggerating."

"Says you. . . . Hey, are you gonna meet me there? Is that what this is all about? I mean Cass, we don't have to go to such lengths. . . . Joseph won't know—"

"Shut up!"

Eddie climbed into the driver's seat and unlocked my door. I didn't open it. He looked at me through the smashed window, puzzled. *Go*, I said wordlessly. He shrugged, started the car, and backed out of the space. I watched him drive off. A moment later Harrington followed him out of the lot, leaving me free.

Four o'clock. Sunset less than four hours away. I still had a lot to do before it was time to catch up with Tommy.

25

Two o'clock in the morning. The street had shut down for the night. I crouched behind the warehouse door and tried to stretch my muscles by flexing. It didn't work. The feeling had drained out of them hours ago. Better than pain, I thought. Keep still.

Behind me, I couldn't see a thing, just shadow on shadow, floating in blackness. The sky was still gray when I arrived six hours earlier, and even then I could barely make out the collapsed mountain of tires that had lain undisturbed since my last visit. Now there was no light at all coming through the cracked-open door. I had to move close to see out, to discern the rubble that was now a parking lot, and once an old man's livelihood.

A ship's horn boomed on the Bay. I gave in to the temptation to shift position. A mistake. My arm began to ache, the side of my body throbbed. I wanted to prize myself out of that tiny space, stretch my legs, and go home to bed.

For the hundredth time I felt in my jacket for the empty Night Train bottle, pocketed as an afterthought when leaving the office that afternoon. I had depended for protection, foolishly no doubt, on a tiny gun that I had barely learned to use. Now it was gone, and it was a question of making do with available materials.

A scraping broke the stillness. I scrambled to the door and peered out. The street was quiet. Then again, the scraping—from *inside* the warehouse.

I held my breath and willed my heart to stop beating so loudly. In the distance a horn honked, a siren wailed. And the scraping, this time closer, maybe twenty feet away in the darkness. Like a nail on cement. I stared in the direction of the noise. Optical shapes swam in my vision. I was still staring at nothing when something cold and wet touched my cheek.

I recoiled in disgust, but the thing found me again, prodding at my face. It snuffled with excitement, as the gleam of an eye caught the light. A dog—one of the strays. I had reported their presence to the SPCA after my last encounter; they had found nothing. They hadn't looked very carefully.

Even in the dark, I could tell that the animal was merely curious, sniffing out this stranger, wanting more information. "Go on!" I whispered. "Get away!" I pushed at the dog; it wouldn't budge. I pushed harder. It growled. I couldn't vanquish the beast without giving myself away. So I sat back and tried to ignore it. The dog settled down with a heavy sigh. It was there for the duration.

I turned back to the street. Now it was 2:20. Malakis is probably asleep in a flophouse a hundred miles away, while I crouch here like a fool. What was my hurry? I should have accepted Michael's invitation to stay.

A shadow moved near the chain-link fence. I craned my neck to get a better view. Nothing changed. Then another movement. Frustrated over my poor vantage point, I slid the door open another inch. The dog sprang to its feet, padded over to me, and sat. Together we watched someone creep along the inside of the fence that bordered the north side of the parking lot. He was carrying something.

He stopped. I withdrew, pulling the dog with me. The animal resisted and bounded back to the doorway. The figure was moving into the lot. Then he was out of sight.

No more activity for what seemed like a long time. I was reaching for the warehouse door to shove it open when a *clank* rang out from across the street. Then a *kachunk*. Metal striking asphalt. The idiot, is he that crazy? Does he think he can dig up a parking lot *with a shovel*?

The noises began to take on a rhythm. First a horrible scraping, then a *kachunk*. Then rocks hitting pavement, and it would start again. Tommy Malakis was trying to get into the basement of the Leeward Inn.

The dog whimpered. I pulled the warehouse door wider, ready to steal across the street and rescue Malakis before his nemesis showed up. If I called out, he would run—and while I could easily catch an old man, the shock and exertion could kill him. I had to get close enough to grab him when he bolted.

One step out of the warehouse and the *kachunks* stopped. I froze. Not a breeze was blowing. Not a sound from the parking lot. Only the hum of the freeway. Had he heard me? I huddled outside the warehouse, praying I wasn't visible, straining to see through the chain-link fence.

An anguished cry ripped through the silence—then was choked off. Then another cry, even briefer, and that jarring scrape of shovel blade on asphalt. Finally, as I crouched in the dirt, a sickening *whump*, like somebody pounding a sack of flour.

That jolted me into action. I leapt up, knees screaming at the sudden movement, and dragged open the heavy sliding door to reveal the searchlight mounted on wheels, rented from Creedy's Spectaculars. It had taken nearly three hours to track down Creedy, but he had hauled the light over with no questions asked, thanks to an extra twenty-dollar bill.

Now I was groping for the switch, so easy to find in daylight, so ridiculously impossible in a dark warehouse when a man is being murdered fifty feet away. The damned dog kept getting tangled in my legs. I found the toggle and flipped it. Nothing. I swore and kicked at the generator. It turned over and hummed to life. A stream of light shot skyward. I jumped on the lens, swiveling it downward, so the beam was pouring across the street.

The fence links threw wicked shadows on the white-haired zombie standing like a rock and staring into the light. He wasn't even trying to shield those cold, pale eyes. At his feet a body was slumped.

"Geraghty!" I yelled. "Cops are coming!" It was the best I could do under the circumstances.

Geraghty lurched to life, moving toward the street. I wasn't sure whether he could see me or not. The generator sputtered, the light flickered for a second, but the current continued to flow. Geraghty was coming on, a huge and mindless moth. He burst through a hole in the fence and broke into an irregular lope.

Things weren't going as planned. I was supposed to intercept Tommy before Geraghty did, then run to my car and get us the hell out of there. Now I had a psychotic coming after me, and a dead or dying man on the other side of the street, and nothing but an empty wine bottle for defense. My only option was obvious. Retreat.

I did—into the warehouse. Right away I knew it was a mistake. There was no other way out. Still I drew deeper inside, waiting for Geraghty. *Come on, you asshole*, I was thinking, trying to psyche myself up. *Come on, sucker.* The dog stood behind the light, growling loudly now. He's protecting me. I've been given another weapon.

Geraghty filled the door frame. He moved faster than I thought. He was trying to shield his eyes and see beyond the light. With a vicious snarl, the dog sprang for his neck.

It must have shocked him, the beast flying out of the light that way, and Geraghty was thrown off balance. He flailed at the air as the dog leapt again and again, pushing him back from the entrance. The fourth time it leapt, it didn't come down: Geraghty had the animal by the neck and was holding it aloft. Dog and man were caught in the tremendous beam of the searchlight, Geraghty trying to keep the snapping jaws from his throat, the dog's legs thrashing. Any one of those lunges could have come away with a mouthful of flesh. The snarls were deafening; not even a grunt came from Geraghty. Finally with one tremendous effort he elevated the writhing beast above his head and twisted its body into an unnatural shape. The animal gave out a strangled cry as its neck snapped. I heard it clearly, the clean breaking of

174

bone. Geraghty hefted the now-limp body and tossed it away in contempt.

He turned toward me with a quizzical expression. The searchlight must be blinding him. He started forward, feeling his way. My only chance is to freeze, hope he'll pass me. Then, when the path to the door is clear, I can make a run for it. Assuming he isn't looking at me right now. I just can't tell.

Geraghty was ten feet away and still coming. My body made the decision for me: it refused to budge. Fear nailed me to the spot. Yet I found myself reaching for a tire. Too heavy to make a decent weapon. But I couldn't go for the wine bottle in my jacket without making a noise. It was just a toy anyway; the idea that it could damage this behemoth would have been funny at another time.

Six feet away. My fingers felt the inner rim of the tire, looking for a grip. Should I throw it or swing it? I had this ridiculous image of a cartoon character rolling the tire at an army of pursuers and scattering them like tenpins. Geraghty was solid flesh and muscle. The "weapon" would just bounce off, assuming I could even throw it that far.

Geraghty was even with me, three feet away. He stopped. To blink would be to broadcast my position. His eyesight was coming back. In one second he would be able to see and I would be dead. Then my foot slipped on a tire, and he saw me.

I burst out of the crouch, hand glued to the tire. It rose, propelled by the force of my entire body, and caught Geraghty in the stomach. *Whump,* it went—a hopelessly weak sound. The weapon flew out of my hand, pitching Geraghty's bulk into a pile of tires. He was tangled up. I grabbed another tire and brought it down on him. It bounced off. Geraghty sank into the pile, arms and legs pumping comically. I staggered past him, and he clamped a hand around my ankle. I couldn't reach another tire, I was about to lose my balance. If I fell . . .

With my free foot I kicked him in the head as hard as I could. That broke his grip. Stumbling against a stack of tires, I pulled it down on him and ran.

I shot out of the warehouse and into the beam of light, making for the chain-link fence. I had no illusions about having incapacitated him. Geraghty didn't look like the kind of man who would go down with a single kick in the head from a tennis shoe.

I shoved through the fence hole, tearing my jacket. Got to get to Tommy. Dear God, let him be alive.

I threw myself on the prone figure and turned him on his back. It was Harry Cremmins.

He seemed dead. No time to check his pulse. I looked over at the warehouse. Now *I* was blinded by the searchlight, my own weapon turned against me. Geraghty could be lumbering across the street at this very moment.

A sound came from behind. Standing against the wall of the neighboring building, trapped in the searchlight's glare, was Tommy Malakis—a.k.a. Max. Just standing there, arms at his side, looking at me and the body of Harry Cremmins. One hand clenched in a fist, like before. Wearing the same clothes as yesterday. To him I was a silhouette. He looked unconcerned, like a boy at a prom too shy to ask a girl to dance.

"Hello," he said cheerily. "What can I do for you?"

"Hello, Tommy." I was trying to keep the panic out of my voice. "It's me, Cassandra Thorpe. From the clinic yesterday? I want to help you."

"Oh, no, I'm here to serve *you*. What'll you have?"

I edged toward him. Malakis stood his ground, mouth crinkled in a smile, watching through those invisible eyes.

I held out my hand. "Let's get away from here. Go someplace where it's warm. Please?"

Malakis shook his head. "I like it here just fine." But he seemed uncertain, as if he didn't recognize me. I took his hand and was about to respond when a shadow loomed on the wall before us, ten times its normal size. Geraghty, breaking the beam of the searchlight, was loping across the street. "Oh Jesus, Tommy," I cried. "Run!"

"Where are we go—" I grabbed his arm and tried to drag him away from the wall. The shadow was shrinking as Geraghty drew closer. Tommy held his ground. I yanked at his sleeve. At last he seemed to understand, and we broke into a clumsy trot, side by side, holding hands.

"Goddamn it, Tommy!" I screamed. "Run, goddamn it!" I shoved him through a hole in the fence on the east side of the lot and we were in the street. Risking a look back, I saw Geraghty extricating himself from the jagged fence links. I grabbed Tommy's hand again and off we went.

Darkness was our only advantage, and it was darker to the north, so we headed that way. Tommy tripped on some railroad tracks; I kept him from falling. The tracks slashed the street on the diagonal and disappeared into blackness. Maybe a shortcut to the next street. I steered us into it.

We were treading on gravel and glass, objects shattering beneath our feet. We might as well be crawling. It was like one of those nightmares where your legs are mired in sand as something terrible draws closer and closer. I collided with a shopping cart, but now it was Tommy's grip that kept me upright. We trudged on through the pitch-black railyard, lights of the Bay Bridge looming ahead.

The shortcut ended at another street, one block closer to the bridge, empty like the previous one. Not a soul around at two in the morning—and no phone booths. We had to make it to the piers, where a security guard was bound to be on patrol.

I pulled the old man across the street and to the right, zigzagging our way to the waterfront. East, north, east. "What you want me to see?" he wheezed. "I'm way too old for this."

At the next corner I got up the guts to look back. The graveled shortcut was cloaked in darkness. It took a couple of seconds to make out the figure of Geraghty moving doggedly, with an easy, side-to-side motion, like a speed skater. He was coming fast. I looked around in desperation. Which way to go? Follow the rail tracks.

We cut north again—to a dead end. To the left a wall, to the right the half-demolished brewery, one side torn away, exposing the floors. Straight ahead, a couple of tank cars rusted at the end of the tracks. Beyond them towered the rocky hillside that was foundation for the bridge. No time to think. I pushed Tommy toward the brewery. "But I gotta go now," he said with irritation in his voice. "I gotta get back to my bar."

"Shut up!" We plunged into the building.

The ground-floor walls had been ripped out, exposing pillars, insulation, and twisted wires dangling from the ceiling. We ran through patches of light and dark, navigating around stacks of junk: window frames, broken chairs, oil cans, bicycle wheels . . . deeper and deeper we went, like mice in a crazy man's maze. All the while I was searching for something to use as a weapon, anything, because I knew we couldn't keep running. It would kill Tommy. I knew I would have to face Geraghty. Alone.

We scampered beneath the skeleton of a staircase and huddled beside a pillar, offering precious little concealment. The shadow of Geraghty moved at the far end of the room, 200 feet away, and he began picking his way through debris. Everything was tinged in soft white light. The moon must be rising. No longer would we have the protection of the dark. This is it. I can't keep him away any longer. I scanned the junk on the floor, still seeking a weapon. Everything was too heavy, too light, too unwieldy. . . . Geraghty burst into yellow light. He had lit a match. Shadows flew around him weirdly, the bare wires projecting like giant spiders. My hand touched something mushy. Animal droppings. I wiped it on the pillar, beside a chalk drawing of a snarling rodent caught in a swath of moonlight. KING OF THE RATS, somebody had written.

Tommy started to speak. I clamped a hand over his mouth. He was still trying to mumble something, his asthmatic wheezing loud enough to attract Geraghty by itself.

"Listen to me," I hissed. "Shut the fuck up. Don't say a word. If you talk or make a noise we will die, do you understand?"

I was choking him. Why doesn't he shut up? Why won't he help himself? He gasped like a dying man, as if someone was repeatedly sticking a knife into his lungs. "It's all right," I said. "You're going to be all right." And took my hand away from his mouth.

Another match snuffed out, leaving only the brightening moonlight. Instinctively I closed my eyes. Like a child. If I can't see you, you can't see me. I looked. Geraghty was drawing near. He lit another match. Then Tommy found it necessary to speak, his voice booming across the room.

"It's my place," he announced. "It's always been mine. You tell him I ain't gonna sell." Geraghty blew out the match.

The psychopath shoved aside something heavy and came toward us. I hauled Tommy to his feet and pushed him up the rickety staircase. Pure reflex. I was consumed by panic. I *can't* fight him off, I thought. Got to keep running. I couldn't see the top of the stairs. Don't think, don't stop. Fear was taking over.

Halfway up the staircase Tommy froze, suspended high over the floor. There were no handrails, nothing to stop us from plunging into the glass and rocks and shit below. "Move!" I commanded, striking Tommy on the back. My body swayed. *Don't look down*. I looked down. The floor moved. Geraghty was scaling the staircase, a dozen steps away, using one hand to steady his ascent. A box was cradled in the other arm. Ten steps. Eight steps. Six. . . .

I kicked out, catching Geraghty in the throat, and he slid backward, his free hand grabbing at the receding steps. My other leg collapsed and I plunged after him.

My arm got jammed in something and broke the fall. My bad arm. I stumbled to my feet and clambered up the steps again. Tommy had disappeared.

Into the blackness I climbed, legs aching, lungs screaming. *Don't look back*. I reached the top. There was Tommy. Just standing there, all aglow in the moonlight. In a long, long corridor with a window at the end. A dead end, of course. With thick metal doors on either side. I grabbed Tommy. Which door? Any door.

It hardly mattered, they all went to the same place: nowhere. We were in a room. No, not a room, a huge concrete vat. A storage tank. Filled with junk, stacks of wood, rags, construction materials. . . . No way out. Panic began to rip through me, lodging in my throat, all-consuming. Cass's last stand.

I heard Geraghty enter the corridor. Matchlight danced past the open door. I pulled Tommy to me. Whispered, "Don't say a word. Don't even breathe." And kept backing away from the door, feeling in my pocket for the empty bottle. Tommy whimpered.

A metal door scraped, a match lit with a *scritch*. How many matches has he got? That would be the first door. Which door had we taken? The third, the fourth? Darkness again. Another door, another match. Scrape. *Scritch*. Light. Slowly I pulled the bottle from my pocket. Scrape, *scritch*, light. Scrape . . . our door. He stood in the doorway. Hello. *Scritch*.

The shock-white hair glowed orange, that blank look fixed on us. In one hand he held the match high. In the other he gripped a metal cannister.

I knew that can. I saw it beside the body of Harry Cremmins. What's he doing? I thought dully. Really I wasn't thinking at all. Just standing between Tommy and this madman. Clutching a twelve-ounce wine bottle.

"Oh, I know what you're sayin'," Tommy said to no one. "It used to be a helluva lot livelier. Hundreds of ships in the harbor. Sailors comin' through, tellin' stories. . . . I got postcards from 'round the world. There they are, up on that wall." Just a nice, casual conversation to while away a dull evening.

I smashed the wine bottle against the wall, leaving a stump of jagged glass in my hand. I'll have to get in close to do any damage. Fine. Call it rage, or blind fear, or even insanity—but I was moving forward, not back, thinking only one thing: *You won't touch him. You won't harm this old man.*

Geraghty reacted too. The arm with the metal can shot out, spilling water. I moved closer. It swung again. Now some of the water was on me. But not water. Greasy . . . smelly. Gasoline. He was going to burn us. The match went out.

Liquid splashed me in the dark. Dripping down my

clothes. . . . Gasoline filled my nostrils. I backed away. *Got to stop him from lighting another match.* So I stepped forward. Tore at the air with my weapon, but air was all I felt. Again the room burst into light. I gripped the glass shard, waiting for an opening. He threw the match.

It landed at my feet, dying before hitting the pool of gasoline. In those seconds of darkness I moved to the right, trying to catch him from the side. Another match flamed to life in his fingers. He saw that Tommy was unprotected and went toward him.

The old man stood at the back wall. "It ain't the same no more," he was saying. "Buildings goin' up all over the place . . . oh yeah, people asked me to sell, but I like it here, I *like* it. . . ." The words were coming a little faster now. As if he knew something was wrong. Only he couldn't quite figure out what. . . .

I lunged toward Geraghty, slashing with the bottle. He careened backward as his match went out. Had I hit something? Maybe just his sleeve, I couldn't be sure. I knew he was starting for Tommy again without bothering to light a match. I heard a sloshing. Again I struck, trying to maneuver between them. I collided with Geraghty, stabbed at the darkness, pushed him away. But he had my jacket, and was drawing me to him. I tried to shake his grip. A splash of gasoline hit me right in the face. I gasped for breath. I was getting dizzy from the fumes. Losing concentration. A third time I lashed out, and I connected with something, for Geraghty made a strangled spitting noise and let go. One second later he had managed to light another match.

"Thirty years I've worked it," Tommy was gibbering, now huddled in the corner, "me and my wife, Leona, she's helped me, she's the heart and soul of this place, you know that, everybody knows that. . . ."

Geraghty snarled. The first sign of emotion. His neck was shiny with blood. The gas can lay leaking at his feet. If he dropped the match now, we'd all go up in flames. He tossed it. I jumped back. It bounced off me harmlessly. Already another match was flying toward me. He was throwing them as fast as he could light them, in one smooth movement, strike and throw. Goddamn fumes. He was toying with me, enjoying the torture, a sick game to this lunatic. I bent low, swinging the bottle like a scythe, while Tommy chattered away. Geraghty got too close, and the bottle ripped the front of his jacket. *Next time it's your chest, fucker.* He grunted and threw another match. It hit the floor at my feet and exploded.

I toppled backward, away from the blaze. It was reaching to the ceiling, a roaring curtain dividing us from Geraghty but trapping us in the corner. My jacket caught fire and I tore it from my body. As I threw it away, it burst into flames.

Tommy was twisted into a fetal position, hands pressed over his ears, screaming. I raised him up. Still he screamed. Now my arms were binding him tightly, his shocked and filthy face pushed against me. We turned around, turned as the flaming figure of Gerald Geraghty came bursting through the wall of fire. We leapt aside and the big man crashed into the back wall. His body writhed on the floor, struggling to get up.

The tomb was filling with noxious fumes. Impossible to breathe. Heat was searing my eyes; I felt light-headed, euphoric, didn't want to move. But there was room to squeeze by to the door if we hugged the wall. Tommy was limp and silent in my arms. I slid along with my burden in agonizing slowness, foot by foot. Holding my breath, fighting to concentrate, swallowing smoke . . . almost to the door. Geraghty rose and came lurching toward us. His jacket and shirt were burnt away, his face black and melting in the heat. I shoved Tommy out the door as Geraghty grabbed me, slamming me against the wall. I bounced back, sent him flying into a smoldering pile of debris, landed atop him and rolled off, got to my feet, rushed into the corridor, swung the groaning metal door shut, and jammed the latch into place.

I staggered away from the vat and fell to the floor, exhausted, beside Tommy Malakis, who lay unconscious, maybe dead. His hand was stretched before him, the one that was always clenched tight, only it was open now. In his palm rested a large coin with a hole in the middle. It glittered in the light from the window. From within the locked vat came a muffled explosion.

We lay there for a while, in the cool light of a rising moon, choking on dust, lungs burning, while the contents of the locked room sizzled into ash.

26

The smell of salt water floated on the night air, and waves slapped at the pilings. On the bridge above, cars flowed, into the city, out of the city . . . going places. An orange moon hung over the Oakland hills. Two very small people were huddled on a bench at the water's edge, beside a phone booth. A shivering old man, barely coherent, clutching his arms. A young woman, maybe thirty-five, no jacket, auburn hair blackened by smoke, face smeared with dirt, blood, and gasoline. Her arm around his shoulder. A passerby—had there been one at 3:30 in the morning— might have taken them for a pair of derelicts. Street people.

"I . . . I . . . woke up," the man was saying, almost to himself. "The . . . room on fire . . . fire everywhere . . . I ran, called for help . . . but it was gone. . . ."

"The Leeward," I said. "Your home."

"Twenty-three years. She died years before that. In the end she didn't know me. But I didn't leave her. I held her hand. Sat with her. Holdin' her. . . ."

"She was beautiful."

He nodded. No tears in those sunken eyes, although he was shivering. The night was clear and mild.

"Then he came after you," I said. "After the fire. The man with the white hair. Where did you see him?"

"Everywhere. All the time. On the street . . . starin' at me, just starin'. . . ."

I knew that stare. The look of a man who could nurture an obsession for revenge for thirteen years. "But you got away."

"A man hit me. In a park. Took away my sleepin' bag. No-good street trash. Never worked a day in their lives, none of 'em did. Always on the street, always askin' for a handout. Get a job, I said."

This from the same man who used to let bums sleep in his doorway out of pity. Then one day he was one of them. "But when that man stole your sleeping bag . . . what did you do?"

"I ran . . . caught a bus. Had a little money, but I lost it and the driver kicked me off . . . I just kept runnin'."

The man who stole the bag, whoever he was, paid for it with his life. A bully who thought he could take what he wanted from the weak. But he was just another link in the skid row feeding chain. There's always a bigger fish.

"And Harry Cremmins," I prompted. "You thought he was gone. Then one day you saw him again."

"That bum!" For the first time there was real emotion in his voice—disgust. "He was a drunk. I kicked him out. Told him, 'Don't come around my place no more, you bum.'"

"But then you saw him—"

"Somethin' I dreamed. That's what it was. Far away from here. Somebody pushed me off a curb. Then I couldn't remember no more. I went to sleep."

With a single shove at the Ukiah bus station, Cremmins made sure that Tommy wouldn't get to San Francisco before him. Maybe he even thought he had killed Tommy. In any case, he was free to assume Tommy's identity. The "treasure" was all his.

"That was *my* place!" Tommy cried out.

"I know," I said, holding him tighter. I was thinking about another man who staked everything on a place that looked insignificant to the outside world. A man filled with pride and love, whose goodness and sympathy left him defenseless to the victimizers. My father.

In the distance a siren wailed, coming closer. Tommy

looked confused. *Not again,* he must be thinking. There were sirens when his bar burned down and his life ended. And when he lay in the middle of a street in Ukiah, a thirteen-year-old nightmare suddenly revived. And now, when he was an old man with his precious illusions destroyed.

The ambulance came flying down the Embarcadero and skidded to a halt before us. Paramedics swung open the doors and extracted a stretcher. "Tommy," I said. He didn't respond. I held out the shiny coin with the nail hole in it. "Here. This is yours."

His mind was far away, unreachable through those black sockets. The spell of lucidity had passed, perhaps forever. He looked at the strange object in my hand and furrowed his brow.

"What is that," he said tonelessly. "I never seen that."

I pocketed the coin as the medics laid Tommy on the stretcher, pulling a blanket over him. He was still shivering as they strapped him in.

Somebody placed a hand on my shoulder. "You called?" I nodded.

"Come on," the medic said. "Better hurry. The old man looks bad."

I shook my head. "I'm all right. I'll see a doctor later."

"Be sure and do it." They loaded Tommy in the ambulance and sped off. I watched it disappear. Reached into my pocket and held the wafer-thin coin up to the moon. Even in the poor light I could see that it was made of something cheap. Tin, maybe aluminum. I bent the coin in my fingers. Last surviving remnant of a treasure.

Another siren approached. The police. I got out of there before they showed up.

A shower felt wonderful, even though my bruises stung from contact with the scalding water. Never mind. Tommy was safe—if not sane. I kept flashing back to the image of a cheap coin nailed over the bar. It probably began as an intentional fairy tale, a way to drum up business at a rundown waterfront dive. Somehow, as his sanity began to slip away, the story of a buried "treasure" became real to him. It came to stand for all that he had lost—his wife, his livelihood, his pride. The treasure was the bar itself, and that was irretrievable.

After two nights without sleep I was past the point of exhaustion. That was fortunate, for the ordeal wasn't over. At nine o'clock Louis Boudeaux's ultimatum would come due. By then I must know what I was dealing with.

The sun was breaking over the Bay as I sat at my kitchen table and spread out the felt pens for the final time. Red, orange, yellow . . . time to decode the rest of the diary. Here we go, Sherman. Now I'll know exactly what you were trying to tell me.

Tuttle was obsessed with the prophets. His keys, which changed every page or so, were based on thundering pronouncements about Judgment Day, evil punished, the coming of a vengeful Messiah. There was the quote from Jeremiah 50:36: *A sword is upon the liars; and they shall dote: a sword is upon her mighty men; and they shall be dismayed*. And Isaiah 13:6: *Howl ye; for the day of the Lord is at hand; it shall come as a destruction from the Almighty*.

As for the deciphered messages, they seemed to be a painstaking recitation of South of Market life, much of it centering around The Wayside. There was a bit more about the Anderson Valley Clinic, and Malakis: "He is hiding here away from the evil on the outside and I will protect him from the evil. . . ." And a lot about Michael Sloane: "A man like a snake in a cave he is concealing millions and the experiments turn good men into evil men. The lies protect him from the light. Today he stayed in his office till noon then he went to City Hall. I know what they do there I have seen them. Mail, junk mail and magazines but it could be a code. Took another picture, him and the men in suits. . . ."

What turns "good men into evil men?" Drugs? That could be the Boudeaux connection. But why did Tuttle start spying on Boudeaux? I kept going. There was mention of the times that Tuttle had been thrown out of The Wayside. And a constant flow of irrelevant observations on everything from government to space travel: "Today the president said he will talk to the Russians about the bombs. I do not think he will talk . . . except on the red phone. . . ."

On and on the diary went, damning Michael Sloane and everyone else who ran a church or a shelter, discoursing on politics and the "invisible web." That was one of his favorite themes. Occasionally he would include a term or two from Boontling: *big book* for the Bible, *high heel* for cop, *tuddish* for mentally impaired. Referring to others, of course.

But I was nearing the end of the notebook—coming now to mention of his meetings with me ("She too schemes away behind me and tells the snake everything")—and I began to realize that I wasn't going to find what I was looking for. Or rather, that I *had* found it in an indirect way. For in those two hundred pages of varicolored ciphers crammed into every line and bursting over the margins into the fold, there was not a single mention of Louis Boudeaux.

I needed time to think.

There were other loose ends in the Malakis case. The weak point was Whaley. The Leeward burns down, Whaley skips town with his mistress, and his wife immediately sells the hotel to a mysterious buyer. Some coincidence. Only Emma Whaley could clear up the mystery.

Another visit to Emma would have the additional advantage of escaping Boudeaux for a while longer. I was out of the house by 7:30, and no one appeared to be following as I headed down the peninsula. Over the radio came the story of Harry Cremmins, dead in a parking lot, apparently struck by a shovel found lying nearby. Strange—all along I had expected him to turn up dead. Now he was, almost as an afterthought.

The radio also spoke of a mysterious fire in the abandoned brewery beside the Bay Bridge, where the charred body of a man was found locked in a concrete vat. I couldn't repress a cold smile on hearing the final detail: his body was too badly burned to permit identification at this point. Police were investigating. A hell of a night South of Market.

I knew what the missing news item was, and so did the police, in all probability: an unidentified old man who appeared to be suffering from amnesia, picked up on the Embarcadero in the dead of night, just two blocks from that brewery blaze. He was accompanied by a young woman who phoned for help but refused medical assistance; she is being sought for questioning.

The house looked the same—the shutters and the vines, the big shady oak, the quiet suburban street. I rang the bell and waited a long time.

She looked surprised and more than a little dismayed to find me on her porch.

"Yes?" Like before, the door was open just enough to let a cat squeeze through.

"Mrs. Whaley, it's me again, Cassandra Thorpe? May I come in for a second?"

"What do you want?"

"Only a bit of history. You remember. About the hotel."

Emma pulled back the door. "I was just taking a nap." Her hair wasn't mussed at all. Same scene: dent in the easy chair, teacup on the side table, fire in the fireplace, seventy-five degrees outside. And that air of antiquity that was depressing and comforting at the same time. Yellow light bled through the discolored window shades.

I sat on the couch and struggled to come up with an opening. What do you say to an old lady whose husband was a fraud and an arsonist? There wasn't time for subtlety.

"Mrs. Whaley, do you know Tommy Malakis?"

She gave it the right amount of thought before shaking her head. "At least not that I can remember."

"He used to own a bar in San Francisco called the Leeward Inn. Does that ring a bell?"

"I hardly think that I would know him if he was a bartender. . . ."

"Bar *owner*, not bartender. Your husband knew him."

"Oh? Was he a friend of Virgil's?"

"You couldn't call him a friend. Virgil once tried to buy the bar from Tommy. That was just before it burned down."

"Virgil never said anything to me about him. Are you certain you're thinking of the right man?"

This is going to go over real big. "We think Virgil burned

it down," I said. Old lady drops dead of heart attack; ex-public defender held.

But she showed no signs of distress. "Excuse me?"

"Mrs. Whaley . . . this isn't easy for me to say. But your husband . . . well, there's evidence to suggest that he was implicated in that fire. I mean, right after the bar burned down Virgil disappeared, and I know he ran off with another woman—"

"He did nothing of the sort!" That piqued her more than the allegation of arson. She sat up in the chair, bristling with indignation. "Miss Thorpe, I really don't understand *what* you're doing here. You say it has something to do with the hotel, but instead you ask me these questions about my husband . . . and these terrible accusations. . . . Would you please leave now? I don't want to talk to you anymore."

There it was—that fiercely protective attitude whenever the subject of Virgil Whaley was brought up. But those bare walls . . .

"I'm sorry," I said. "That was cruel of me—"

"Of course it was cruel! Now I have asked you to leave—"

"I have to talk to Virgil."

"Virgil is dead. My husband is dead. He never looked twice at another woman."

"How did he die?"

"Young lady, you have a perverse curiosity about the tragedies of other people, don't you? You say you're a public defender?"

"I was, yes."

"And you defend criminals? People like you are the reason it's not safe to walk the streets at night. And then you have the gall to accuse my husband of being a murderer! I don't understand."

"What do you mean, a 'murderer'?"

"Those are *your* words, not mine."

"No, they're not. I never said anything about a murder. I said Virgil was suspected of burning down the Leeward Inn. Somebody *was* killed in that fire, but I didn't mention it."

"You *are* a lawyer. Trying to trap me. Well, I am not listening to a thing you say. Would you *like* me to call the police?"

190

"Okay, fine." I stood up. "But if you don't tell me who bought the Doyle Hotel, and what happened to Virgil, then you may be charged as an accomplice in a murder. There's no statute of limitations on murder."

"I won't be threatened."

"I'm not trying to threaten you. I want you to see that a crime has been committed and the criminal is still at large. Walking the streets, as you say."

"What concern is it of yours?"

I had failed. To this woman I was the enemy, as were all public defenders, probably all lawyers. Of course, it hadn't helped to march into her house and call her husband a crook.

"At least think of Virgil's reputation," I pleaded. "He is the only suspect in a murder. We know someone else was involved. If you could only tell me that. . . . Just say who bought the Doyle. . . ."

She gave out a little laugh. "Public defenders. Who are you defending now?"

"The victims." Same as always.

"And what would you know about that?"

It was unbearably hot in that impersonal living room. Why was I wasting my time berating this poor woman? In a way she was just like Tommy Malakis—living out her remaining years in solitude. Everyone has a different way of coping with the pain. Fixed forever in Tommy's mind was the image of a lovely young girl in a summer dress. But what about Emma? How did she remember her husband? Certainly not by photographs. By killing him in her memory, not by keeping him alive.

"Did you love him?" A shocking question, and I knew it the moment I asked it. But I couldn't stop the words.

"You have no right!" She was fumbling with a pair of glasses, unsure whether she should put them on. "When you're older you'll understand . . . you learn to live with your loss. Just because you don't let it show . . . that doesn't mean . . ."

She put the glasses on and took a handkerchief from her purse, kneading it in her lap. Her mouth continued to move for a second or two. It was an unconvincing performance.

There was something cold about the way she held her chin in the air, like someone whose honor had been questioned, not her love.

"Please tell me who bought the hotel," I said again. "You know how important that is, don't you?"

This time I wasn't asked to leave. She knew how falsely her emotions were playing. As if she had acted a part brilliantly up to now, but suddenly, in the middle of a crucial scene, had lost the essence of the character. Now she was the shell of an actress. And the audience knew it, too.

"Do you know what that hotel is like?" she said, not looking at me.

I nodded.

"The dirt . . . the rats . . . the scum who live there, have you seen all that? One day we broke down a man's door. Not a sound from him for nearly a week. There he was, lying on the floor . . . covered with *flies,* where do all those flies come from when the windows are closed? And the bums, complaining about food, about heat. And the drug dealers. Fifteen-year-old children on heroin, oh, yes, I saw them, shooting up in the bathrooms. I pleaded with Virgil to sell. Not even to sell, to get *away* from there, who cared about getting any money for that horrible place? But he never would. Always said he was about to make some *real* money. Any day now. Any day now."

The words came out with a chill that sliced through the stuffy room. Biting, vengeful . . . she hated Virgil Whaley.

"And then Tommy Malakis came along," I said, hoping not to break the spell.

She took off the glasses and wrapped the handkerchief around them. "Virgil was going to buy the property and split it, half and half. We would be rich, he told Virgil, a big development was coming and the value of the land would go up five times, ten times, maybe more. But the bar owner wouldn't sell. Virgil wasn't the one who burned it down, but when it happened, he knew he was out of the deal. So he tried blackmail. Said he had him under control. Said the man had no choice but to pay Virgil, or Virgil would tell the police." She laughed again, but there was no humor in it. "My husband was a fool."

Suddenly I was fighting off nausea. A silent partner . . . someone whom Malakis wouldn't know was involved . . . a genius at working behind the scenes, at pulling other people's strings. Whom Malakis might even take to be an ally. . . .

"Michael Sloane," I said. "It was Michael Sloane, wasn't it?"

She looked at me with surprise. The handkerchief was folded neatly in her lap. She spoke slowly and matter-of-factly.

"He would have killed me too. I knew that. Instead he offered me money for the hotel. Lots of it. I could get away, he said, where I would be safe. Never breathe a word to anyone, and I would be safe. Fixed for life." She smiled. "Just like Virgil used to say, only Mr. Sloane *meant* it. It was Virgil's fault anyway. I didn't think twice. He gave me my only chance to escape."

Emma sank into the armchair, arms tucked at her side. Clutching the handkerchief, eyes closed. The only sound in the room was the muffled ticking of the purse-size travel clock on the table beside the exhausted old woman. The bare greenish walls stared at her in the yellow light; the furniture was scraps of alien sculpture. I left her alone. Time to call Louis Boudeaux, and tell him that I had what he wanted.

27

Full house at the Cleveland Memorial Baptist Church: people overflowing the pews, sitting in the aisles, jostling for space in the vestibule. Closing night for Michael Sloane. His final chance to confront the evil developers, to save South of Market from the hotels, office complexes, tennis clubs, design studios. In the eyes of the neighborhood, he was the star attraction, and the show was about to begin.

Several long cafeteria tables covered with paper formed a makeshift dais in front of the altar. Half a dozen men in business suits faced the crowd, with pitchers of ice water before them and diagrams on posterboard arranged on easels. All men, all in their thirties, all wearing expressions of deep social concern. Slickly dressed women were moving down the aisles, passing out "fact sheets." The church had been turned into a boardroom.

I was standing at the back. Through the rustling of paper and disparaging murmurs of the crowd it was difficult to hear what the suits were saying. "Revenues to the city . . . allowances for low-cost housing . . . we respect the unique character of South of Market, we want to *build* on that . . . thousands of jobs . . . affordable parcels . . . want to work with you . . ."

I felt a hand on my shoulder. There stood Saint Michael of

the Slums, in people's work shirt and blue jeans. "The party line," he whispered. "Do they really expect us to swallow this shit?"

I shrugged. "People can be pretty gullible sometimes."

"Where the hell have you been?" he asked, putting an arm around my shoulder. "I was worried sick when I read the papers yesterday."

"Hiding." It wasn't safe to go home yet. Leaving Emma Whaley the day before, I had sought shelter at Sonia's house. There I had slept for thirteen hours, and could have slept for thirteen more. Except that I had an appointment to keep.

"Cass, what happened the other night?" Michael asked.

"What do you think happened?"

"I haven't the slightest idea."

"Didn't they ask you to identify the body in the brewery?"

"Why should they?" he asked. "Was it Malakis? God, tell me he's still alive."

For the first time I was watching Michael at work from the outside, and it was a chilling experience. He really seemed to believe what he was saying.

"Somebody you know," I said.

"Well, tell me, damn it. I'm about to go on. Who killed those guys?"

"Why don't you ask Emma Whaley?"

Applause broke out in the room. Michael's face went rigid, his jaw locked, and his eyes drilled through me. He removed his arm. Everyone was clapping wildly, beaming at us. No, just at Michael. They were ignoring me. It was his turn to speak. The developers had had their say; now Saint Michael would tear them to pieces. Only he didn't look well. The blood had drained out of him, and he was just standing there, his back to the altar. A couple of people tried to steer him toward the front. Finally he backed away, still staring at me, his mind making desperate calculations. I returned the stare, and it was he who broke the spell by turning and walking to the dais.

There he went, savior of the neighborhood—and owner of several valuable parcels of real estate. His strength was an intimate knowledge of other people's weaknesses. They didn't know they were doing his dirty work. Tommy Malakis had to die, and Gerald Geraghty wanted revenge for the death of his friend, so Michael brought them together—with my help. Sherman Tuttle was a nuisance, so Michael convinced Louis Boudeaux that Tuttle was spying on the drug dealer's operations. As for me, he must have had a great time manipulating my emotions—first stubbornness, then anger, then affection. What was Tuttle's word for him in Boontling? *Silent fister*.

He had reached the microphone. He stood over the table of businessmen, glaring at them. Today, at least, he would have no problem creating the right emotion. He had simply transferred that look from me to the men at the front.

"That's a lot of fine talk," he began. "We see these pretty charts and drawings, and we hear about all the money everyone's going to make, and what a *great* thing this is for the neighborhood. Of course it's great. You think these gentlemen would be here today if it wasn't great? Only problem is, it's not so great for you. What's so great about fifteen square blocks of hotels and condos and furniture showrooms? Where are all the jobs for *us*? Are they going to hire us to paint the pictures for their art galleries? Oh, sure, maybe a few of you can be maids in the big hotels, if you don't make too much trouble. But I'll tell you something, brothers and sisters: when these people come in, we go *out*." He shook his head mournfully for effect. "Ain't gonna be no room for the likes of you and me."

On he went, pacing it perfectly, talking of displaced people and "gentrification." It was as if he had already forgotten our encounter of a few minutes ago. Michael Sloane had the ability to get so far down inside himself that for the time he spoke, he became one with the audience. A case of temporary sincerity.

Even from the back of the room I had no trouble hearing his words. They carried that far and beyond, to the people in the vestibule, and maybe to the street, too. I couldn't deny that I had been drawn to this man, invigorated by his charisma and his sense of commitment. It wasn't the first time

196

that I had been fooled. Eddie Thorpe was a great-looking package when I married him, despite my father's objections: handsome, funny, rebellious, nice ass, Protestant. How is it, I wondered, that I can understand the psychology of judges, juries, cops, prosecutors, and street people, and be such a lousy judge of men?

Michael was building to an impassioned climax about the homeless and the hungry and the mentally disturbed. The suits at the altar were shifting in their seats, downing too much ice water. One of them, I now realized, I recognized: a man with an impeccably trimmed beard and a razor cut. He was in one of Sherman Tuttle's photographs, talking to Michael at The Wayside.

Michael saw them at the same moment I did, the two tall black men in tight pullover shirts, blocking the exits. No, three—one was up front, guarding the door to the sacristy. None of them took his eyes off the speaker. Michael didn't miss a beat. The words were still coming, but he was looking toward the doors. Beneath that flow of rhetoric a silent communication was going on. *Take your time*, the men seemed to be telling him. *We can wait*.

The speech ended to a churchful of applause and a standing ovation. Michael pushed into the adoring crowd, looking over his shoulder. The guard at the altar was a few feet behind. Straight ahead was me, and the two others. Michael milled about, seeking the crowd's protection, but they misunderstood his intent and stepped aside to give him a nice, clear path down the aisle. He came toward me, and as he drew near his face twisted into a look of hatred—mouth parted slightly in a smile, eyes smoldering behind half-closed lids. The look of a stranger.

The black man caught up with him and whispered something. Michael nodded. Maybe the bravado was just show, too, because he seemed to be having a hard time keeping his shoulders up. As he went by, the guard at his side, he mouthed something through that half smile that I didn't catch.

I wanted to shout back, but I was interrupted. One of the

197

guards, a bouncer type about six feet four, was standing beside me. "You come too," he said.

I shook my head, safe in the crowd. "No. That wasn't the deal."

He had a hand in his coat pocket. Soft words, hard to hear. "I'll kill you right here."

He smiled warmly. I smiled back. It's okay, I thought. This shouldn't screw things up. I hope. Go with him. He followed me into the vestibule.

Nobody was paying any attention to us. I could run. Would he really fire through a crowd? How far would I get? I looked around for cops. None. Don't worry. Be cooperative. Nothing's going to happen.

It took a few moments to adjust to the bright sunshine. Hot today. The glare bounced off the street. A derelict in sunglasses was stretched out on the steps of the church, hands behind his head. He was humming. Parked at the curb was the van with the beautiful deep purple paint job, the lovely little mountain scene on the side. The back doors were open. The bouncer prodded me down the steps. We moved toward the van. The motor was running. Last opportunity. Run now, chance it.

But I didn't run, trusting to the situation. I let myself be led to the back of the van. Inside, on a seat running lengthwise, sat the other two guards, 250 pounds apiece. Between them was Michael Sloane, looking small.

"Get in," the man behind me said. I stepped up. He gave me a hand. A gentleman.

My escort stepped in behind me. I took a seat opposite Michael and the two others as the doors slammed shut. My eardrums felt a momentary pressure. Air tight.

"Glad you could come," Michael said.

"Shut up." That came from the front. There were two other men in the car, both black—the driver, built like the bouncer types, and a passenger. He was the one who had spoken. It was a familiar voice.

"Let's go," he said, and the van began to move. I watched the church recede through the smoked windows, and the people going by, oblivious. I can see you, you can't see me.

The man in the passenger seat didn't turn around. He was smaller than his companions, maybe five eleven or six feet, with a slender build. From the back I could see only a white linen blazer and white trousers. His hair was cropped short, straightened, and spiked.

"Where's the book?" he asked, still without turning around. The voice wasn't so friendly as before.

"I told you. There's nothing in it about you. You're safe from Sherman Tuttle."

"Bullshit. I'm safe from nobody."

"Look, it's Sloane you have to worry about, not Tuttle."

"Why don't you let me decide my own worries?" To the driver he said, "Left at the next corner. To the warehouse."

Michael spoke to me. "This whole thing has kind of back-fired on you, hasn't it, Cass?"

I didn't respond.

"I mean, you try so hard to cut a deal with Boudeaux to have me wiped out, then this happens. Sort of defeats the whole purpose."

I shook my head. "Puts you out of business. Your partners are going to wonder what happened. They *are* your partners, aren't they? Sunrise Development, I mean."

He shrugged.

"But they're in Hong Kong. And they need somebody who lives *here*—who's got a finger on what's going on every second. Our Man in San Francisco. You know—'this guy's about to sell out, this one won't sell, this one's place just burned down and we can buy it for cheap.' Of course, they probably didn't know the details behind that, did they?"

Michael just smiled.

We were headed south, past China Basin and into an area of warehouses and machine shops. Nobody following. I turned to Boudeaux. "Don't you see what he does? He suckers people. He suckered you. Started spreading the rumor that Tuttle was spying on *you*. Michael set the whole thing up. And you finished it off for him."

Boudeaux turned around for the first time. Beautiful brown eyes, almost kind. A flattened nose that might have been broken a couple of times. And a mottled chin, suggesting that he had a tough time with razors.

"No one suckers me." He smiled. His teeth were terribly crooked and pushed out of shape. "Just look around."

We drove in silence for a few minutes. Finally Michael spoke again, calmer this time.

"Cass here doesn't understand a lot of things." He was addressing Boudeaux. "Spends all her time hanging out with winos, and she doesn't even see how much all of this is worth. Completely blind."

He looked at me, shaking his head. "In ten years this neighborhood is going to be . . . transformed. Cleaned up. I mean, look at it now, what do you see? Filth, and garbage, and poverty, and bums. I used to live in New York. It's the same here now. There's nothing worth saving, why can't you see that? Because you are blind. But just wait. It's all changing." He leaned toward me. "It's going to be *better*. That's what you don't understand. It's *redevelopment*. Everybody wants it this way. The bums, they'll just go someplace else. They always survive."

"And you thought you would hurry things along a little, by burning down a bar or two."

"Oh, come on!" Michael cried. "It was *happening*, land getting snapped up right and left. They got the whole South of Market all laid out, right now! We're just a small part of it. I mean, there was Tommy Malakis, sitting in his miserable little shack in the middle of a gold mine!"

"Too bad Virgil Whaley couldn't share in it."

Michael didn't answer.

"That was a big mistake, using him."

"Fuck that," he said, with sudden savagery in his voice. "I don't get many people wrong. I had you pegged. Shitty little bleeding heart. You were so fucking tough, strutting around the courtroom. Different on the street, though, isn't it? Nobody to hold your hand. You just fall apart, like that." He snapped his fingers. "And you try so hard, that's what cracks me up. All for the bums. The lousy, stinking bums."

I flew out of the seat and went straight for the viper's throat. I never got there. One of the guards stuck out an arm and slammed me back into place. I sank into the seat, rigid with anger and pain, imagining Sloane in bloody pieces. For him, money was a pleasant bonus. It was the manipulation that he really enjoyed.

We turned at a block-long warehouse, into a narrow street. Then another turn, and suddenly we were driving down an alley flanked by high walls. It was a dead end, a receiving dock, and it seemed to be deserted. The driver pulled up the emergency brake and cut the engine. "Okay," said Boudeaux. "Let's do it."

Now, I thought. The cops are going to show up now. I looked out the back window, expecting to see twenty squad cars tearing up the alley. Here comes the cavalry. But they weren't coming. Had they lost us in traffic? The whole thing was arranged so carefully. Boudeaux nabs Sloane, cops nab them both. They hadn't counted on me going along, but that shouldn't make any difference. Where the hell were they?

"Hold it," Michael said. "Listen to me, Louis. You are about to make a *big* mistake."

"I don't think so," Boudeaux replied. "You see, I don't appreciate being used in the way that you have used me. You have dragged me into your personal affairs, but once I am dragged, I stay there. Understand?"

What are they going to do, I thought, shoot us right here? Somebody is bound to hear the shots. There are people around. Then the thug on Michael's left drew a switchblade.

"Damn it, that's my whole point," Michael was saying. "You're involved whether you like it or not. So why not take advantage? There's millions of dollars at stake. And no reason why we can't work together."

Wonderful. Now they're going to gang up and kill just *me*. I wonder where the police are?

"Millions of dollars," Michael repeated. He could be excused the rhetoric. He was talking now for his life.

"I'm telling you Louis, the arrangement is perfect," he continued. "Think of the connections for *you*. Hong Kong, man. Investors with a shitload of idle capital on their hands. The chance for expansion. You'd wipe out your competition easy. *I've made that connection, and it's yours.* Right now."

Louis laughed, but I couldn't tell whether he thought anything was funny. "Real easy. Just like that."

"Yeah, just like that. And only one thing standing in the way, then we'll be free to operate." They didn't bother to look at me.

Michael would be free, that is. And Emma Whaley and Tommy Malakis would be dead.

Now all three of the henchmen had switchblades. "It's simple," Michael said.

"Simple," Boudeaux said.

"That's right."

"I work for no one. Particularly for no honky."

"We work *together*. You're still in charge."

It was working. Boudeaux was going to let Michael go. Only I had to die. Just me. I looked down. The floor of the van was covered with a plastic sheet. I hadn't noticed it before. My stomach churned. I felt cold all over. Right here. Right now. For the first time I understood that I wasn't going to be rescued. Something had gone wrong. I had walked right into it, thinking I was so smart. Now it was happening, it was really happening.

Boudeaux nodded at Michael. Then at the three men with carving knives. Then he looked at me and shook his head. The rear door was locked. Besides, I couldn't budge. My body was freezing. No pain anymore. It was just draining away. The man beside me took my arm. Draining onto a goddamn plastic sheet. . . .

Something struck the side of the van, struck it hard, like a torpedo. The van rocked. Everybody froze. And listened. Then again, another *wham!* on the side of the vehicle. And again, this time smacking the back doors.

"Hey!" somebody yelled from outside. "Open the door!"

I couldn't see anyone. Louis looked like he was trying to stare right through the body of the vehicle.

"Come on!" the voice called out. Now a head appeared in the back window, trying to see in. His nose and fingers were pressed against the smoked glass. Scraggly beard, uncombed hair, dirty face. A derelict.

Boudeaux put a finger to his lips. The man beside me placed a cold blade across my throat.

The derelict was yelling random obscenities, stopping only to throw himself against the van. Inside, we were mannequins, not daring to breath. Boudeaux stared calmly at the ceiling, waiting it out.

The face returned to the rear window, hands cupped around his eyes. The glass began to fog.

I wanted to cry out, beg for help, or just scream until they stopped me. Was he sane enough to figure it out? Would a filthy street person, who was probably rousted by paddy wagons three or four times a week, call the cops?

The knife blade was warm now against my skin. I could lunge for the door. But I would leave my throat behind.

Then he was gone.

Silence. Still nobody moved for another minute. I could sense the muscles of the man next to me relaxing. And mine getting tighter. It was a brief stay of execution. Boudeaux turned half around to give the order. He was stopped by the noise.

Some sounds grate on you a certain way, make your jaw shiver—fingernails on a blackboard, a fork on a napkin. And the scraping of a sharp object on metal, like the body of a car. That was the noise exactly, a continuous nerve-wracking *screeeeech* as something rudely gouged the van's side, its flawless purple paint job.

This was too much for Boudeaux to bear. "Open it," he commanded, and the henchman closest to the door lifted the latch and pushed it open.

The swinging door knocked the derelict on his ass. He scrambled to his feet and thrust his filthy face into the van.

"Excuse me, sirs, but your pretty little vehicle happens to be parked right on my sleeping bag!" he shouted. "I'm minding my own business, and all of a sudden, you drive up and you park right on it! Now what are you gonna do about it?"

"Shit," Boudeaux's henchman said.

"Get him out of here," Boudeaux commanded.

The man started crawling under the van. "Will you look at this!" we could hear him saying from below. "It's got *tire marks* all over it! Son of a *bitch*!"

His feet were protruding from beneath the van. He

grunted, legs thrashing in the dirt. He was trying to pull the bag free.

"Just close these doors and we will drive somewhere else," Boudeaux said. "We're running out of time."

I threw myself at the door and broke the grip of the thug beside me. Another one tried to block me but I moved too fast. I came flying out of the van and landed face first on the ground. The man under the vehicle chose that moment to back out, and he collided with my pursuer, who was just climbing down. "Murder!" the man yelled. "Assholes!" He flailed about, swinging at the huge henchmen, who had me by the leg. The other two bounded out. I kicked free, jumped up, and hauled off down the alley. Here we go again. Gasping as I ran. *Can't get caught. Got to get away.* I hear them behind me. Got to make it to the street. To safety.

I ran right up to a police car. Difficult to avoid hitting it. Then another. And a third, screeching up to the alley entrance, lights revolving. Cops were everywhere. The henchmen stopped. Boudeaux, Sloane, and the driver were still in the open van. The usual warnings: hands up, don't move, got you covered, you have the right, etc. One of the cops asked me if I was okay.

"Where the fuck were you!" I screamed. Didn't feel very polite.

"Waiting for you to give the signal," he explained, baffled. "You were going to tell us when the van took off."

"You idiot, I was *in* the goddamn van!"

"Well, we figured that out, but we didn't know right away. . . ."

I shook my head with disgust and started looking for a nice corner in which to throw up for the third time in three weeks. The derelict who had saved my life came trudging down the alley toward the cops. "About time!" he said in a squeaky voice. "They were gonna get away! Parking on my sleeping bag like that—"

He looked at the cop cars, now six of them, for the first time, and his jaw dropped. "Jesus H. Christ," he said. "It's just a lousy sleeping bag. . . ."

They were bringing Boudeaux and Sloane down the alley, both men handcuffed. They got separate cop cars, Boudeaux first. One of the cops said something to Boudeaux that made him mad, but before he could react he was shoved into the car.

Then it was Michael's turn. He didn't look back as he climbed in. I leaned against the wall and watched him go. There was a terrible taste in my mouth, and I wanted water. The car drove off.

South of Market was losing its fiercest, most dedicated champion.

28

In the matter of *People Versus Cassandra Thorpe*, the charges were as I expected: assaulting a police officer, possession of a concealable firearm, possession of a loaded gun in a public place, disturbing the peace, resisting arrest, practicing investigation without a license. I sat in the judge's chambers with Sonia, who was my lawyer, and a district attorney, a particularly obnoxious man whom I had battled on a number of occasions. I had spent the last week and a half recuperating. Again.

"These are serious charges, Miss Thorpe," the judge said. He was one of the nicer ones: he liked me because we were both Italian.

The judge had the file spread out before him. "Hardly appropriate behavior for an officer of the court. I mean, it just builds, doesn't it?"

Sonia spoke up. "Your Honor, I believe it should be taken into account what results my client got from inadvertently breaking a few small laws. She ended up apprehending some people whose crimes were substantially worse than her own. A hell of a lot worse."

"Watch your language in my chambers, counsel."

"Sorry, Your Honor."

"We'll let it slide." He turned to me. "You made a few

mistakes, didn't you? Do you honestly think that all of this is erased by your good intentions?"

"I don't know, Your Honor," I said. "I guess that's for you to judge."

"Very funny. Now the D.A. has made an offer—"

"Yes," said the D.A., an overweight, middle-aged, under-endowed man. "We'll let her plead to resisting arrest for six months suspended, two years' probation, and a fine of a hundred and fifty dollars. And we'll dump the rest."

I wasn't being charged for the death of Gerald Geraghty. That was clearly self-defense, and the chief district attorney, who had higher political ambitions, didn't care to publicize the fact that a killer had been walking around South of Market for thirteen years. The police, handed the answer to the murders of Sherman Tuttle and a John Doe in a sleeping bag, were happy with what they had. And Officer Marty Kessler would be still able to bear children.

"Your Honor," said Sonia, "my client cannot afford even a misdemeanor charge—"

"All right, all right, now listen," the judge said. "This is the offer that I will accept. Miss Thorpe is required to perform an extended period of community service. Let's keep it open-ended at this point."

Sonia bristled. "I have *never* heard of such a thing."

"Neither have I," said the judge. "But in this case we'll make an exception. The community service I have in mind is private investigation."

"Your Honor?" I said.

"You are required to apply for a private investigator's license and use it, Miss Thorpe."

"I already have," I said. "The application went in two days ago."

"Then we have no problem, counsel?"

The D.A. broke in. "Absolutely, I would say there's a problem, yes—"

"Howard," the judge interrupted, "leave it alone. She did a good thing, and now she's going to pay for it."

The D.A. put on his hangdog look, but said nothing more.

"I'll have to consult with my client," said Sonia.

* * *

The two men were standing below a billboard advertising a fast-food chain.

"'America's Meat and Potatoes.' That ain't no meat and potatoes! That's a hamburger and french fries! Your meat and potatoes is your steak, your baked potato—"

"Uh-huh. Or sometimes, you, you, you, you get your boiled potato—"

"Or your little *red* potato."

"With some sour cream and chives."

"And wine."

"That's right, with some fine wine. . . ."

They were still discussing it when I entered Wilma's. Sonia and Joseph were sitting at a table in the corner.

> Well, lace up your boots and walk on down
> To a knock-down shack on the edge of town
> There's an eight-beat combo that just won't quit
> Keep a-walkin' till you see a blue light lit
> Fall in there, and you'll see some sights
> At the house, the House of Blue Lights.

Early Times was in energetic form, banging away on the piano and singing in his raspy voice while part of the crowd kept time as they drank, and the rest just drank. Joseph ordered another round of beers. It was Friday evening, five days into autumn. Starting to get cold again.

"Most of all, I like the way Cass got rid of Eddie," Joseph was saying. "That was the best part. Of course he ain't got a helluva lot upstairs for brains, but still, it was somethin'."

"You must really love the guy," said Sonia.

"Joseph just has his own way of showing it," I said.

"You're a sweetheart," Sonia told him.

"Yeah, well, I'll tell you one thing, and you can believe it," said Joseph, tapping the back of one hand against the palm of the other. "That's the *last* time I let Cass here get herself beat up by anybody. Come to think of it, you gave me the slip too. Well, it won't happen again. If you're stickin' around this slum, you're gonna get some protection, like it or not."

"I'll let you know." That was all I needed—Joseph blundering around with good intentions on every case that came my way. *In the meantime, relax. You're home.* That morning I had called Sara Ludlow to tell her I wouldn't be moving to Santa Rosa. She was less surprised to hear the news than I was. It was the final thing to do before getting down to work.

At first I felt only relief—that the pressure of the Malakis case was finally off, that Michael Sloane and Louis Boudeaux were in jail. But there was apprehension too. There would be no apple orchards and rural scenes, no lifetime spent preparing the wills of farmers and drawing up contracts for wineries. Just filthy streets and wiped-out derelicts, little fish on the feeding chain. Waiting for the next earthquake.

Tommy Malakis was recovering—at least his body was. He had lapsed into a merciful amnesia. Soon he would be transferred from the hospital to a halfway house, where someone would look after his needs. As for the Sunrise Development project, it was still rolling along, without Michael Sloane's assistance. There was just one change in plans: the owners were naming the hotel "The Gold Doubloon," after the pitiful piece of tin that Tommy had clutched in his fist for thirteen years. Local color, the builders called it.

"I can get you a wonderful deal on some business cards," Sonia was saying. "And this weekend we have *got* to buy some paint for that office of yours? Elroy can help too, when he gets out of jail. He'd be great, sloshing around with a brush? Provided he can balance on a ladder."

"Good luck," Sara Ludlow had said to me that morning. "You made the right decision." All I could think of was a peaceful home in Santa Rosa, fading away. I had cut off my safeplace. Emma Whaley still had the shell of hers; Tommy Malakis would never get his back. And the people who had hung around on the edge of Tommy's dream—Sherman Tuttle, Harry Cremmins—had paid for it. There wasn't any safeplace at all—no place where the derelicts didn't have to confront the cold reality of the world, where they didn't have to scrape for food and cigarettes and Night Train, and boxes in which to sleep. Down here it was the Depression, all the time.

A young burnout was wobbling in the doorway of Wilma's. Hair hung over his eyes, and his T-shirt was in shreds. Under his arm was a dirty bedroll. He stood there for a long time, listening to the music, a song about a safe, warm world where you can eat and drink as much as you want, where there's a bed for everyone:

> There's fryers . . . broilers . . . Detroit
>   barbecued ribs.
> But the treat of the treat
> Is when they serve you all that fine
>   eight beat.
> You'll want to spend the rest of your brights
> At the house, the House of Blue Lights.

Early Times was really rolling now. The whole room was moving in rhythm to the music, eight to the bar.

Sonia's briefcase landed on the counter with a thud. She flipped the latches. "All right," she said. "What have we here? We have a hooker rousted in Union Square for the fortieth time, a crazy who stripped naked and hung out on the jungle gym in the park for three hours, a wino who stole a car and drove to a bar . . . right through the bar, I mean. . . ."

The files piled up before me and I began leafing through them, the latest recitation of crimes committed by the dregs of society, my clients. The wiped-out man in the doorway stood for a few moments more. Finally, with a supreme effort and the support of the doorjamb, he turned, shoved the bedroll under his arm, hitched up his pants, steadied himself once more, and lurched out to the street.